"Undress me, J...

"With pleasure."

The two simple words rocked Nathan to the core: he could get off on her voice alone, he thought. The fire between them was daunting.

Somehow she managed to undo all the buttons on his shirt while he kissed her deeply, his hands everywhere. He couldn't stay away from her as she peeled his clothes off and shed the rest of hers.

Within moments they were both completely bare. She was even lovelier than he'd imagined. Curved and full, she was beautifully formed, her skin a satin olive tone that bespoke her Italian heritage. *Maria indeed.* The dusky aureoles of her nipples accentuated perfectly rounded breasts with velvet brown tips that would be heaven to taste.

"You're amazing," Jennie said as she stepped forward, pressing against his painfully hard shaft.

"I was just thinking the same about you," he whispered. Emotion swamped him.

The mood had shifted, and she looked at him, open and vulnerable. Conflict suddenly twisted with passion in Nathan's gut—how could he make love to the woman he was secretly investigating?

Dear Reader,

Who doesn't have a few secrets of their own, right? But most of us don't have secrets like the ones Jennie Snow and Nathan Reilly are keeping. She's a former mafia princess turned cop; he's investigating her on the sly, all the while fighting his attraction to her.

I knew when Jennie Snow popped up on the pages of my last HotWires book, *Flirtation,* that she had to have her own story. Jennie needed a hero with a nature as passionate as hers, as well as someone brave enough to help her face her past and her future. Good thing Nathan Reilly showed up. This book explores some of my favorite themes—family, deception and dealing with the past. And as Jennie discovers, we're all fortunate when we find someone to stand by our side when we face difficult moments.

Now that Jennie (using her real name, Maria, again) and Nathan have headed off to Boston to head up a new HotWires office, look for more books featuring new members of the team. Stop by my Web site www.samanthahunter.com, or drop me a note to find out what's coming next.

Happy reading,

Samantha Hunter

HIDE & SEEK
Samantha Hunter

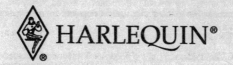

HARLEQUIN®

TORONTO • NEW YORK • LONDON
AMSTERDAM • PARIS • SYDNEY • HAMBURG
STOCKHOLM • ATHENS • TOKYO • MILAN • MADRID
PRAGUE • WARSAW • BUDAPEST • AUCKLAND

ISBN-13: 978-0-373-79271-9
ISBN-10:   0-373-79271-9

HIDE & SEEK

www.eHarlequin.com

Printed in U.S.A.

ABOUT THE AUTHOR

Samantha Hunter lives in Syracuse, New York, where she enjoys the luxury of writing full-time for Harlequin Books. When she's not writing, Sam likes to work in her garden, quilt, cook, read and spend time with her husband and their dogs. *Hide & Seek* marks her sixth Harlequin Blaze novel to date. Her first was *Virtually Perfect*, released in 2004. Most days you can find Sam chatting on the Blaze boards at eHarlequin.com, or you can check out what's new, enter contests, or drop her a note through her Web site, www.samanthahunter.com.

Books by Samantha Hunter
HARLEQUIN BLAZE

*The HotWires

For Milene, Jane and Vivian.
"The bird a nest, the spider a web,
[wo]man friendship."
—William Blake

1

JENNIE SNOW GRIMACED over the top of her laptop screen, trying to focus on the work in front of her but failing miserably. Nathan Reilly was to blame. He stood outside the windows of the climate-controlled HotWires offices, deep in conversation with a detective. She couldn't take her eyes off of him.

Though it was uncomfortably cool in the office—the computer crime labs were kept at low temps to protect the machinery that populated the room—she became uncomfortably warm every time she glanced in Nathan's direction. He was hard to ignore.

Nathan wasn't overly tall or burly like so many of the men she'd grown up with—he had a nice, solid build and was just the right height to meet her eyes when they shared a level glance. If she were held against him, all of their important parts would mesh perfectly. And meshing with Nathan was becoming more of a possibility, though she'd been struggling hard to deny it.

He'd been seducing her for the past three months

with his sexy glances and clever conversation. Not to mention the flowers he kept sending her. They were never the same type of flower. Nathan always managed to surprise her. However, the accompanying card always asked the same question: "When?"

She'd put him off for as many good reasons as she could think of. First off, he was five years younger than she was: twenty-eight to her thirty-three. Plus, he was relatively new to the job, having only been with HotWires for under a year, and he was busy building his career.

Lastly, Jennie never formed close romantic ties with any of the men she'd known, and there'd been a few over the years. She wasn't a nun. Still, she couldn't allow herself to become involved in anything more serious than a casual relationship. For a multitude of reasons. Though Nathan was getting more and more difficult to resist.

She pulled absently at the soft cashmere neckline of her sweater and heard a distinctly female chuckle come from the desk to the left of hers. The chuckle was sarcastic as hell, and Jennie knew she'd been caught in the act of lusting openly.

Sarah Jessup-Sullivan, one of the original members chosen to join the prestigious computer crime unit, followed Jennie's gaze with a mischievous, knowing look, and laughed again.

"You've got it soooo bad for that man. He's hot stuff. Admit it."

"I'll admit no such thing. You just go for Irish guys."

Sarah sat back, crossing arms over her stomach, which was back to being washboard flat even though she'd just given birth not quite two months before.

"Only one, thank you very much. Actually, before Logan, I was much more attracted to the macho Latin type, Italians, Hispanics. I'd never dated an Irish guy, though there are plenty of them in the city. Logan was my first."

"And the last. The only."

"Yeah."

Jennie smiled at the soft look that warmed Sarah's face as she spoke of her husband and baby. Sarah wasn't an overly sentimental woman by nature, but marriage, and then motherhood, had smoothed her rough edges without making her any less formidable. Sarah was one of the toughest cops Jennie had ever met, yet she somehow managed to preserve her hard-ass image in the department even when she showed up wheeling a stroller and carrying a diaper bag.

They were the only two female members of the unit. The HotWires—a nickname reflecting the group's high-tech specialties—had been around for almost seven years. It had been started by Ian Chandler, who was still the head honcho of the group. He'd hired them all. Not only was the unit expanding locally, there was also growing demand for similar units across the country. Ian had his hands full, but stayed in the thick of it even as his job involved more and more administrative duties.

And while Jennie enjoyed close friendships with her male colleagues, it was nice to have a female friend around, even if Sarah was frequently gone on assignment. Jennie didn't work out in the field very much; she'd had the training, but her expertise in mapping crime was more useful in the background of the action. If Sarah was Batgirl, Jennie was more like Alfred.

Having Sarah back was great. Jennie knew that while Sarah loved her baby, Caleb, she was thrilled to be back in the saddle again, too.

"It's great that Logan has the time to spend with Caleb so you could come back to work so soon."

"I know—his shop is doing well, and he loves being Mr. Mom."

"He's so devoted to you both, you're lucky. Don't you miss being home, though, just a little?"

Sarah appeared thoughtful for a moment, and shook her head resolutely. "I went crazy for the two months I was home. I love them both to bits, but I felt like I would crawl out of my skin if I couldn't get out of the house. Logan is much more of a homebody."

"It works then. And he's not upset about the risks you have to take in this job?"

"Sure, it still comes up now and then. But he knows I wouldn't be happy doing anything else."

"Quite the man you found."

"You said it. I love him, and I love that he can understand how much I love my work, too. Not all women are so fortunate."

Jennie nodded, not entirely sure she completely understood, but pleased for Sarah anyway. Jennie loved her work, too, but that was because it was all she had. Marriage and family were out of the question for her. If she had what Sarah had, she might quit and contentedly stay home, baking cookies and taking walks in the park…enjoying her children and making a home for her family.

She sighed, and pushed that fantasy aside. Right now, she should be concentrating on bringing Sarah up to speed on current cases.

Sarah, whose sharp observation skills missed little, caught her ogling Nathan again.

"That poor guy has been after you nonstop for months. When are you going to give him a break?"

Jennie grinned, knowing her answer was going to set Sarah back a few feet.

"Friday night."

Yup, she thought with satisfaction, as Sarah leaned in, her hand grasping Jennie's forearm.

"Are you kidding me? You two are finally going out on a *date?*"

"It's just dinner."

Jennie couldn't help smiling, though she remained conflicted about going out with Nathan. On one hand, she had a very good list of reasons why this shouldn't happen. However there were two very influential items that undermined all those good reasons: one, she liked him; two, she was lonely.

Jennie was used to attracting a certain amount of male attention. Sometimes she even enjoyed it. She had the normal urges that healthy women had, and she liked to work them off with a good-looking guy from time to time. And Nathan certainly fit that bill. But maybe she'd made a big mistake accepting his invitation to dinner.

She might be fooling herself that she could keep this under control. She enjoyed having a nice no-strings-attached relationship with a man occasionally. But she'd just celebrated her thirty-third birthday—alone. The years were slipping by, and what did she have to show for them except her work? Her work was challenging, and it helped her deal with her past and feel as if she was making a difference in the world. All the same it didn't keep her warm at night, that's for sure.

She considered another good reason to cancel the date—the problems a romantic entanglement could create in the office. She'd already had an affair with one of her colleagues, though that had been over for years. E. J. Beaumont was now a happily married man. Jennie was good friends with his wife, Charlotte, and was godmother to their second child, Annie. A relationship with Nathan would be hard to keep under wraps in such a small unit, and Jennie didn't want to start being known as the office good-time girl. In a police station, where women were so outnumbered, it was important to keep your professional image intact.

Nonetheless, Nathan was just too good to resist; and in truth, his pursuit of her, the flowers—and the seductive glances those amazing gray-green eyes cast in her direction when she was least expecting them—had finally crumbled the fortress she'd built around herself. There were several ways to access a system, Sarah always said. You could take a subtle and stealthy approach; you could wage an all-out attack, or you could convince the system or the people who ran it to give you what you wanted.

The last option, social engineering was Nathan's specialty.

With dual degrees in psychology and criminal science, he could have had his choice of any number of good jobs within regular law enforcement. He'd done his doctoral thesis on how computer hackers exploited the human element of technology, using human habit, weakness and error to get what they wanted. Hackers took advantage of one human trait in particular: the tendency to trust others. People were inherently trusting; they wrote down their computer passwords because they never really thought anyone would look through their desk or their e-mails. They left the systems open thinking no one would take advantage. They gave the waiter their credit card at lunch thinking the young man or woman would never steal the number when they were out of sight.

Nathan had provided a simple example at a recent seminar. A hacker comes to a reception desk, knowing the name of several people in your office, their office numbers and even things like the fact that someone just had a baby. He or she says they've come to deliver a baby gift, and asks to come by, just to drop off the present. Chances are, you agree. People want to help; they want to trust.

And that simple fact put hackers one step closer to getting what they needed. Once they were in, they could take it to the next step and find their way into company computers, networks. It happened every day.

Jennie wondered if this was what Nathan was doing to her—wearing down her resistance, charming her with his flirting, getting by her barriers because he'd somehow convinced her to let him in. He'd never pressured too much, but he'd never really stayed out of sight for long, either. Of course, she thought of him when she woke up and saw the latest flower arrangement on the dresser. He engaged her in conversation that had no romantic slant whatsoever, but his eyes sent a whole different message. He pursued her and yet waited for her to decide to come to him.

The difference was, she knew it, and she knew herself well enough to be sure she wouldn't give him anything more than she wanted to. She was a mature, experienced woman, after all. Right? But that's what scared her, a little. She'd been alone for a long time, and that loneliness made her vulnerable. Was she only seeing what she wanted to see, or worse, what he wanted her to see?

She shook her head to clear the cobwebs of her thoughts. Hacker talk. Most things in this office came down to hacking, even love. They had to be careful, or they'd be paranoid about everything, and she already had too much of that in her life. She glanced at the poster over Sarah's desk: F.U.D. Fear. Uncertainty. Doubt. It was a hacker mantra, but it also was a real part of Jennie's life. Maybe she'd let too much FUD in over the years.

"So where are you going?"

"Huh?" She'd been caught zoning out again, and felt the color creep up into her cheeks.

"Dinner. Where are you going?"

"I don't know. I told him to keep it casual."

"My first date with Logan wasn't a date, either. It was casual, too."

Jennie rolled her eyes and laughed. "Stop distracting me, please? Let's get back to work."

Sarah's brow creased in consternation. "Yeah, right. I don't think I'm the distraction. But, yeah, okay, back to work, if you can take your eyes off of your Irish loverboy."

Although Jennie enjoyed the banter, she felt the familiar tug of sadness that never quite went away.

She wished, especially in moments when she felt close to someone, as she did with Sarah, that she could tell them the truth about herself.

Sarah had no way of knowing that Jennie's entire life was a lie—her name wasn't even Jennie Snow. Didn't anyone ever notice how strange it was that an obviously full-blooded Italian women had such a WASPy name? But few people ever questioned it.

For those who had noticed over the years, she'd repeated the story she'd been given by the Witness Relocation Program—she'd been adopted. She was an only child, both parents dead. That much usually stopped people from inquiring further out of respect for privacy.

Jennie didn't think about it much, but there'd been a time in her life when all she wanted was to meet a nice guy, have a solid job and have a bunch of beautiful babies. Though she'd gone to college and wanted to have a career, she'd always imagined she would eventually have a full family life.

Until she'd discovered the travesty that was her own family—at sixteen she'd wandered into the small, fenced backyard of their city home to check on some abandoned kittens she'd brought home, only to find several of her male relatives beating some poor man half to death because he'd owed them money, and he wouldn't—couldn't—pay. So they'd seen to it that he'd paid in broken bones and bruises—a message he could take with him for the next time he borrowed more than he was good for.

Her rosy view of life, the idyllic vision of her supposedly close Catholic family, had been shattered. She had never revealed what she'd witnessed, but she'd started noticing all the little things she never had before that night. Her dad, her uncles, her cousins…all belonged to the mob. Everything she'd grown up believing in was a sham.

She'd spent several painful years trying to live with her secret, allowing her parents to assume she remained clueless about the family's ties to the mob, even as she'd watched her two brothers be slowly subsumed into "the life." All she'd wanted to do was get out, get away and forget it all, starting her own life over somewhere else. And she had.

During finals of her junior year in college, she'd gotten word that both her father and her youngest brother, Gino—a gentle, sweet soul who hadn't really belonged in that life—had been killed in a gangland slaying orchestrated by her Uncle Bruno, her father's own brother. Jennie had vowed to do what she could. She'd gone to the FBI, and she'd offered them every bit of information she could in hopes Bruno would be punished for his crimes. In the end, all he'd ended up serving was seven years, and then he'd been paroled for "good" behavior. What a joke.

Jennie had entered the Relocation Program, where she'd changed her appearance, her life and her name.

While they'd wanted to shuffle her off to the Midwest, she'd insisted on staying on the Eastern Seaboard, working for the government as a computer cartographer—a Graphic Information Systems specialist—who mapped organized crime activity. She believed wholeheartedly that her uncle would never look for her right under his nose. For some reason, all the guys thought everyone in Witness Protection headed to the heartland.

Here, she could also keep better tabs on *them.* She could devote her life to helping the authorities stop their activities for good. And that's what her life was about—and at least she had a life, though it wasn't perfect. But whose was? She saw people every day who had worse lives than she did, so she wasn't about to complain.

Her thoughts wandered back to Nathan. How could she ever marry, or have children, knowing that it would all be a lie? How could she ever endanger their lives with her secrets?

Temporary affairs and light engagements—a man in her bed, but not in her life—was all she could look forward to. It had to be enough.

Sarah had no idea, and Jennie knew it made it difficult for her female friends to understand why she cut herself off from love and family. She let them think what they wanted. EJ and Ian were the only other people who knew, or who would ever know. They kept her secret safe. Sometimes it was a relief having someone who knew the truth, someone who could understand, even though she never discussed it.

She'd been living this kind of life for over a decade. Lately, she'd been yearning for more in a relationship. Between sex-only flings and marriage, there were all kinds of degrees of intimacy. She hoped she might find something in the middle with Nathan.

NATHAN STRODE OVER to his desk, sliding the laptop bag from his shoulder and onto the chair, then perused his appointment book and the stack of new files on his desk screaming for his attention. He'd let Jennie presume he hadn't noticed her watching— but every covert brush of her gaze had touched him through the windows that separated them. Still, he couldn't look her in the eye—not yet.

He turned his attention to a seminar he was giving later that week on protecting personal security information—it was astounding how many corporate breaches came down to someone being careless with a password. It was difficult, because part of his work was teaching people to be suspicious, to be conscious of how people might be manipulating them. For the HotWires, he functioned as a kind of "profiler" for techno-crimes.

On top of that, he had no fewer than two critical meetings today. The morning had completely gotten out of control, the new assignment that had just landed on his shoulders throwing him for a loop.

After the unexpected meeting that had waylaid him on his way into the building, he hadn't even known if he could show up at the office and act normally. But Internal Affairs insisted that he needed to keep a regular schedule, not arouse any suspicion. Nathan had to put the skills he studied in others—in criminals—into practice, and lie to everyone around him. It didn't come naturally.

He was still processing what they'd told him, and he didn't want Jennie to figure out that anything was wrong. She'd catch on, though, if he didn't go say something. He never just walked by her, as he did this morning. He was acting out of character already, and he had to get a grip.

He went over to her, hoping he looked casual—normal—but the way his skin prickled and his body hardened just seeing how the soft waves of her dark brown hair rested on her slim shoulders told him he was in trouble. He valued his sense of cool—hard-won in a family filled with quick Irish tempers, but he felt anything but cool right now. One of his grandmother's favorite sayings came to mind: *If you dig a grave for others, you may fall in it yourself.*

"Thanks a bunch, Nanna," Nathan muttered under his breath.

He saw Sarah get up, grabbing a sheaf of papers from her desk before she walked over to him, glancing back at Jennie to see if she was looking. As she came closer, she swatted him hard with the rolled-up papers.

"What the heck are you doing, Junior Mint?"

Sarah was bestowing her best glare upon him, but he stood his ground, used to dealing with his four temperamental sisters. Sarah was a total ballbuster on a good day; when she was after you, look out. Usually Nathan was able to give as good as he got, and he knew that had earned him a measure of respect in Sarah's eyes.

"Motherhood is obviously softening your temperament, Sarah."

"Why did you just blow her off like that?"

"I didn't blow anyone off, Lady Amazon," he used the nickname which Sarah sometimes found charming, and sometimes she didn't—this was one of the times she apparently didn't. He sighed, planting his hands on his hips. "Besides, what do you know about me and Jen?"

The look she pinned him with clearly said *idiot*.

He grinned, pleased that apparently Jennie had been talking about him—it was the only way Sarah could know that he'd finally convinced Jennie to go out with him. He certainly hadn't made an issue of his feelings within the workplace—at least, he prayed he hadn't.

"I know enough."

"Listen, I had a tough morning and I'm just getting myself together. It's nothing to do with Jen. Give a guy a break, will ya?"

Sarah's sharp blue eyes narrowed as if she was dissecting his every thought to see if he was being truthful. And of course, he wasn't. But he wasn't the only one in the office living a lie, either, was he? Everything had become such a frickin' mess so quickly, but he had to get a handle on things, and fast. He didn't manage to do that quickly enough, because Sarah seemed to pick up on his stress, laying a hand on his shoulder.

"You okay?"

He shrugged, piling on another lie. "Just some things at home. It's okay, but it took some of my time this morning."

"Family's important, Nathan—if something's wrong, you can ask Ian for a few days off. He's great about that. Besides, there's nothing major going on around here at the moment."

If she only knew.

Hell, if Sarah knew what he was up to, she'd remove all of his limbs slowly and painfully, and then she'd reassemble them in different places. But he had to get her to back off. He shook his head, pretending to check over a memo left on his desk.

"I don't need time off, I'm just a little frazzled about being late. But everything's fine." He took a step closer to Sarah, making quick eye contact, and whispered, "To tell you the truth, though, I'm a little nervous."

Sarah raised her eyebrows, and she stepped forward, looking him squarely in the face.

"About what?"

Her voice had lowered to a whisper to match his, a common and reflexive phenomenon that happened between people to increase the building of rapport. When you wanted to draw someone closer, you lowered your voice. When you wanted them to give you their full attention, or to be more comfortable with you, matching their tone was the most effective way to accomplish it. Voice and tone were incredibly powerful tools when you knew how to use them, as so many hackers did when they were chatting someone up to get information they needed.

He shrugged, sliding a furtive look in Jennie's direction. "Friday night. We have a date. I don't want to give her a shot at canceling."

Actually *he* was the one thinking of canceling; he'd thought about it all the way upstairs to the office. He'd rehearsed in his mind what he would say, and how he would say it. But in the end, he couldn't bring himself to break his date with Jennie.

Sarah shot him a skeptical look, and Nathan knew he'd been made. "Don't try your little con-artist tricks with me, Reilly." She poked him in the chest, hard, for emphasis.

"I don't know what you're talking about, and...*ow.*"

"Just stop playing games and go say good-morning. The woman hasn't taken her eyes off you since you got here. It's making me nuts how you two are dancing around this—just get it over with already, will ya?"

Sarah turned and strode off, and he wondered

exactly what she and Jennie had said to each other. As he approached Jennie, her scent washed over him. He was so damned attracted to her.

He'd been on cloud nine about that fact until this morning. What he had learned today should have put him off completely, dampened his desire for her—*something*—but it hadn't. He wanted her. Bad.

She had presence and a womanly sensuality that the twenty-something women he'd dated up to this point lacked. He hadn't so much as asked another woman out since he'd set his sights on Jennie, so his long-denied libido was arguing aggressively with his common sense.

He idled down to stand beside where she sat, leaning back against her desk and tilting a little sideways to get her to look at him. It was their morning ritual. A dance of sorts, as Sarah had described it.

His mom had always said that he seemed to like things more when they weren't easy. Probably his stubborn nature, which Ma always blamed on his father. Of course, his ma was twice as stubborn as any of them, though she'd never admit it.

He reached out, pushing a silky curl back behind Jennie's ear. Her breath hitched a little—she wasn't immune to him—and he smiled.

"Hey, gorgeous. Thirty-two hours and counting."

"Morning, Nathan."

He loved the way she said his name, even when

she was trying to sound completely unimpressed. If Sarah hadn't told him otherwise, she could have pulled it off.

He watched her closely, taking in her full sensuous lips, her flawless olive skin and those eyes…he would talk nonsense with her all day just to watch her expressions change, to study how her mouth moved. For a split second, he imagined her full lips moving under his and sucked in a breath.

"Thank you for the dahlias, they're gorgeous, though I have no idea where you managed to find dahlias at this time of year. It must have cost a fortune."

"Well worth it."

"What, just to have dinner with me?" Her tone was one of disbelief.

"No *just* about that."

She sat back in her chair, watching him with a curious gaze. "Nathan, why are you so intent on dating me? You're a handsome young guy. You must have girls falling at your feet."

"But not the one I want. Not yet."

She laughed, and he ignored the emphasis she placed on *young*—he might be a few years younger, but he was more than up to the task of making Jennie Snow feel like the woman she was. To him, the age difference meant nothing. When he was fifty, she'd be fifty-five—so what? Wouldn't matter then, didn't matter now.

As if she could read his thoughts, her expression

became more serious. "Nathan, you know this is just dinner, right?"

Glancing around to ensure no one was listening, he leaned forward. He took her hand and pulled it up to his mouth, where he feathered a kiss over her knuckles, a move that sent fire scorching down into his gut, and beyond.

"Let's just see what happens, Jen. We're attracted to each other. You know it. I know it." He held her gaze, returning her hand with a smile, and saw a slight one of her own form. She couldn't deny the attraction that was between them. She didn't say another word.

He loved what she did to him. How just touching her had wiped his mind clear of everything but the need for her.

All the same there was no way for him to ignore what he had just been informed of—Jennie Snow was not Jennie Snow at all, but former Mafia princess Maria Castone. There was also a chance she was a Mafia mole planted in their department, a spy.

"Nathan, what's wrong?"

He swore silently to himself for allowing his troubled thoughts to show. It could be dangerous for both of them.

"Nothing at all. I guess I'd better get to work before Ian has my ass for getting a late start."

She continued to look at him with that perceptive gaze—the woman could see too deeply; he'd have to be careful. As much as the assignment to investigate Jennie sucked, he didn't want to blow it. With any luck, he had the opportunity to prove her innocence, and he hoped to hell that she was innocent.

He didn't care about her past, who she was. But if she was a mole, if she was passing information back to her family, then they both had a serious problem. Because in spite of everything they'd told him, and everything he knew, it didn't stop him from wanting her.

2

"SO DO YOU KNOW anything new about the *puttana?*"
Bruno Castone stuffed his face with his favorite
rigatoni and sausage, then chewed slowly, intently.
He looked over expectantly at his nephew, Tony,
who winced—just slightly—at Bruno's use of the
slur in reference to his sister. It didn't escape
Bruno's notice.

"What? You have a problem with my language?
She's not your sister anymore, she gave that up when
she ran to the feds, turned against us."

"She might've been pinched. We don't know she
went willingly, Uncle."

"There's no other way to go. She could have come
to me, come to us, but instead I ended up a guest of
the state thanks to her. She took seven years of my
life." He cleared his palate with a glass of Chianti, and
set his fork down on the table a little too hard, repeating his question. "So, do we know? Did you find her?"

"Not exactly, though we have a plan. They've got
her hidden somewhere, deep. We've leaked some information to see if we can flush her out."

Bruno's eyes narrowed. "What kind of information? How come you didn't clear this with me, first?"

Tony shook his head, his tone reassuring. "*Misinformation,* I should've said, Uncle. Don't worry so much. I thought that if we 'accidentally' leaked that we were getting information from inside their program—from someone who was only *pretending* to be a witness—they might lead us to her. We have our inside guy whisper in a few ears, and he'll see what they do with the information. If they think she's been reporting back to us all this time, they'll contact her and, bingo, we find her."

Bruno was silent for a long moment, then smiled widely, satisfied by the news and the pasta. "You're a smart guy, Tony. I always said that's what we need nowadays, guys who have smarts, more than your father and I had. We had to live by wits and fists. You stay on this, and tell me the second anything changes. Paul G. is on my ass, and I don't need one more problem."

"Paul making any moves on us?"

"He's always hemming me in, questioning my every decision, especially since I got out. It's been six years, and he still keeps on me about every little thing."

"Because he never okayed the...hit."

Bruno frowned; his nephew never could talk about the hit on his father and his brother. For a while Bruno had considered taking Tony out, as well, as an added precaution. He was glad he hadn't. Over the years the kid had proven to be an asset, apparently preferring to stay alive over revenge. Smart, like he said.

"Paul's the big boss. I just don't need any more heat from him if any of this goes south. It's your neck on this one."

"You got it."

As Tony turned to leave, Bruno almost stopped him again. Something in his gut bugged him. Maybe it was that small sign of doubt that Tony still was sympathetic to his snitch sister's plight. Or maybe he was imagining things. They were in a touchy business. For now, he'd trust Tony. He picked up his fork, stabbing the pasta ferociously, imagining what he planned to say to his niece before he killed her.

JENNIE HATED THIS. She wasn't the type to fuss over what she was wearing, but she'd just spent an hour and a half trying on every pair of jeans she owned and nothing felt right. This date with Nathan was driving her nuts. She never should have agreed to it. Too late now. He would be here in twenty minutes, and she had no idea what they were doing, or what to wear. She went through her closet one more time.

It was late October, Halloween was only a few days away. The evenings were cool but the colors were still warm; the foliage was close to its peak, reds, yellows and oranges creating the colorful burst before the grays and whites of winter blanketed the city.

This was always one of her favorite times, even

more so than Christmas or Fourth of July. She loved the sweetness of the cusp of the seasons, the bounty of the harvest, the crisp smell of the air. When she was a child, she'd play in huge piles of leaves that she and her brothers would rake next to a hill that sloped down the western side of their home, and when it was big enough, they'd run and jump from the top, landing in a cushion of musty-smelling leaves, delighted. That seemed like another lifetime. Had she really ever had those experiences, or had she just dreamed them?

Shaking off the memories, swallowing the knot in her throat, she grabbed a wool skirt the color of ripe apricots and tugged a white chenille, V-neck sweater over her head. There. She wasn't going to change again, or even look in the mirror, for that matter. She was comfortable, and she'd go with that.

No sooner had she applied her lipstick than the bell rang. She was annoyed at how nervous she was. Her pulse picked up as she approached the door.

Well, maybe she had a right to a few nerves. She was a confident woman, but it wasn't every day that some younger, handsome man was showing up at her door. A man who looked at her with such wicked intentions that she felt like a girl again. She took a deep breath. This was stupid. It was only Nathan, for God's sake.

When she opened the door, her nerves plus a thousand screaming hormones went on alert causing her to go mute. Decked out in dark-gray wool pants and a blue silk shirt, polished from head to toe, Nathan was flat-out gorgeous.

"Maddon'." She lifted her hands to her lips, unsure if she had whispered the familiar Italian epithet or thought it. But, no, she had spoken. Words tumbled from her lips, and they weren't the ideal words she would have chosen, but the brain-mouth connection had obviously broken down completely.

"You're all dressed up. You look amazing. I'm way underdressed. I thought we said we'd do something casual."

"This is casual, and you look amazing, too." He took a step forward, his gaze moving over her so intently she forgot to step back and suddenly they were closer than they'd ever been. She wondered if they'd make it out of the apartment.

"Let me just change this sweater."

She started to turn, feeling like an idiot for needing to escape. Then suddenly she found her hand captured by Nathan's. The next thing she knew, he'd tugged her back against him, so they stood fully flush against each other, her back to his front. She thought she'd stopped breathing, except that she was surrounded by his scent, and he smelled fabulous.

His cheek brushed her hair, and his mouth was by her ear. "You don't need to change. You're beautiful." His lips graced her earlobe and she thought her knees were going to buckle. "You're perfect, Jen."

Although she could hardly think, the one thought that surfaced was that she wished it had been her real name that fell from Nathan's sexy lips. *Maria,* not Jen.

She pulled away, simultaneously aching and panicked at the thought. She could *never* afford to think that way. Jen was her real name. There was no other. Why was her mind torturing her this way, tonight of all nights? She felt oversensitized as if every nerve ending were exposed. She didn't understand why he had such a strong effect on her. It wasn't as if she were some quivering virgin. It wasn't as if he were the first man to touch her, or look at her that way. Yet he felt like the first one—suddenly she couldn't remember any of the others—and that set off danger signals deep inside. She laughed nervously, pushing her hand through her hair.

"You move fast, I'll give you that."

He shoved his hands in his pockets, looking abashed. "I'm sorry. I didn't mean to push. You do look perfect. I wanted you to know I meant it. You always look great. Tonight you're glowing."

He smiled and was transformed from charming to devastating. Was this really Nathan from the office, whom she'd resisted for so long?

He wanted her to believe that he thought she was beautiful? Hell, she felt like the cherry on top of a sundae when Nathan looked at her. Ripe, delicious and as if he was about to pop her into his mouth, whole.

Heat traveled up into her face at the image, and she tried to think of something to say.

"You may want a coat, though. We'll be on the water, and the air could be chilly."

"Okay. I'll just be a minute, then." She excused herself so that she could get a coat, though she was feeling so warm she wasn't sure she'd really need it. For the first time in years, she said a short prayer as put on her coat, asking that she could get through this evening without making an idiot of herself any more than she probably already had.

She walked back into the hall, stopping short, startled to find Nathan wasn't there. She heard movement in the other room, what sounded like a drawer opening and shutting, and headed in that direction—what was he up to?

She found him rearranging some flower vases by the window over her desk, and studied him for a moment before querying.

"What are you doing?" Her tone was sharper than she intended. She didn't say anything else, waiting for his response. He turned, smiling in an embarrassed manner at being caught—caught at what, though?

"Sorry, Jen. I noticed you had these on the table in the hallway. They don't get enough light there, so I just moved them near the window. The blossoms will last longer that way."

"Oh." She wasn't quite sure what else to say, flustered by her first, defensive instinct at anyone touching her things, rummaging around her apartment. It was only Nathan. Still, she thought she'd heard a drawer opening. It must have been him moving the flowers.

She was so rattled, she couldn't be sure what she was hearing. She'd lived a careful life, protecting her privacy for so long, that she didn't know if she could ever trust anyone completely. That well-worn reasoning, however, didn't stop her from feeling ridiculous.

"Are you ready? We have reservations for seven."

She nodded, turning to the door first, though every gut instinct she had told her to wait until he walked out in front of her—why was she being so antsy? She tried to shake it off again, brightening her voice. She was going out with a handsome, younger man for a night on the town. She was just nervous about it, and that was all. She needed to relax.

"On the water? Where are we going?"

"I chartered a private dinner boat—we'll have a four-hour cruise around the Bay. Dinner is provided, we just have to sit back and get to know each other a little better, I hope."

"Ian must be paying you better than the rest of us."

He just laughed, and didn't elaborate. She was touched that Nathan was going all out to impress her—he was really pulling out the stops. Whatever he hoped could come of this probably wasn't going to happen.

It was the *probably* that bothered her—making room for doubt—not so long ago it would have been *definitely*.

He knew how to get under her skin, though it wasn't an entirely uncomfortable feeling. He stopped on the sidewalk halfway to the car, turning her to him, placing his hands lightly on her shoulders.

"Listen, we're just going to have a nice time. No expectations, so relax. I just wanted to do something special for you."

"You do things all the time, the flowers, now this…"

"I do it because I want to, not because I'm trying to pressure you. There is no pressure, okay?"

She felt the knot in her chest loosen a little, and she smiled up at him; his irises were dark in the dusky light of the evening. He stepped a little closer, and she swallowed, feeling her breath come a little faster. Her tongue darted out to moisten dried lips, and he groaned a little.

"I know it's more traditional for the kiss to happen at the end of the date. Let's just get that particular pressure out of the way now, you think?"

She found herself nodding, not entirely of her own volition, though she didn't have much time to think about it. His mouth met hers. It was a gentle first kiss, an introduction, a question and a promise of what might come later. It startled her to realize, when he pulled back, that she wanted more.

Much more.

Damn.

He smiled and took her hand, though she could

see the pulse at the base of his throat beating faster than before. Smiling in spite of herself, she followed him quietly to the car.

"SO YOU HAVE *FOUR* SISTERS?"

Nathan lifted his glass of Chardonnay as if inspecting the color, looking over the top of the crystal at Jennie's features, warmed by the candle lantern on the table between them and relaxed by a good dinner and several glasses of wine. How did she get even more lovely every time he looked at her? The little voice in the back of his head had been sending warnings every ten seconds that he was walking on thin ice pursuing this woman whom he was also investigating. He took another sip from his glass, washing them away.

She was very likely innocent—he'd never seen a single thing in the time he'd worked with the HotWires indicating Jennie was a mole. On top of that, Ian Chandler and E. J. Beaumont were no one's fools. *Unless they knew,* the voice chided. Was he being naive? He wrenched his mind back to her question.

"I'm sorry, I was lost in thought." He set his glass down, unable to take his eyes off her. "Yes, four. Mary, Kathryn, Shelly and Gwen, in that order. I'm the only boy, and the youngest."

She laughed then, her face lighting up. "You poor guy. They must have had such fun with you. Did you find yourself being the victim of dress-up parties at a young age? You must have been like a little doll to them."

He shook his head, grinning. "I learned early on how to defend myself from all that. Dad helped. Said he wouldn't have his only son growing up girlie. Of course, he made sure his daughters could hold their own, so he wasn't a complete sexist."

"So you're the baby. Your parents kept trying for a son?"

"No, they were just really Catholic. No birth control and the like. Mom actually had a few miscarriages in between each of us, which accounts for the intervals in our ages, but I was her last, at forty-two. When I get on her nerves, she tells me they played with the idea of naming me, 'Enough.'"

As he laughed with her at the joke, he studied her carefully, as well. The family life he'd grown up in shouldn't be completely unfamiliar to her—or to Maria Castone, anyway. She'd also been raised in a Catholic Boston family that adhered to traditional values, when it came to religion and reproductive traditions, in any case. It was a subtle form of fishing, a way to find out what was going on under the surface. She didn't bite, however.

She didn't even blink, showing no sign of connecting with what he was saying. She was very good at keeping it all hidden, then again, she'd had lots of practice. The warning voice started humming again, and he shut it off.

"You don't often see large families like that anymore."

"People can't afford them, not that we could, either. It was a stretch a lot of the time, but there was plenty of love to make up for what we didn't have."

"That's nice."

"How about you? Sisters or brothers?"

He thought he saw something flicker briefly in her eyes but then it disappeared—whatever it was, it was sad.

"No, I was adopted. An only child of older parents. They've passed on now."

"So you're all alone?"

When she shrugged, he saw the tightening of her facial muscles, the way she averted her gaze. Whatever the truth was about why she was here, and what she was up to, she wasn't thrilled with this topic of conversation. The pain of the secrets she carried inside, no matter what they were, created a flicker of hope that she wasn't the criminal they were making her out to be.

If she had been separated from her family for all this time, completely cut off through the protection program, he couldn't help aching for her.

He didn't know if he could live the way Jennie had had to live. He wished he could say something, tell her he sympathized. He couldn't. Not yet anyhow.

Her tone was neutral, though, when she replied. Practiced, like a speech she'd delivered many times before. "No, I'm only alone when I want to be. Family is not the only way to fill your life."

"That's true, I suppose."

"You know, I never did ask, but what did you do before you came to the HotWires unit? I know you have psychology and criminology degrees, right? How'd you end up working in a tech unit? Why aren't you out there doing all that profiler work we see on TV shows?"

He paused, unsure whether he should go along with her blatant change of the subject, taking the focus off of herself. But this was a date, not an interrogation. He frowned, hating how business was interfering with what should have purely been pleasure. He shoved thoughts about the investigation aside and went along with her.

"Well, you know I grew up in Boston, and that I'm Irish." He added the last with a smile and an affected brogue he'd picked up from his grandfather, who had been determined to give up neither his native language nor his accent even though he'd lived in America twice as long as he'd lived in Ireland. Grandad used to joke that the accent got him laid twice as often as his American friends without one, and Nathan could confirm that he'd used it in college with similar results.

"I went to college there, no need to move out of the house and spend more money when you have some of the best schools in the country outside your back door. Not to mention the best ballpark in the world."

Jennie arched an eyebrow, but she had a sparkle in her eye that charmed him. "You love Boston?"

Was the sparkle because she'd grown up in their beloved city, as well?

"With all my heart. Miss it, so I try to get back often enough. Have you ever been?" He asked the question with a slight sinking feeling—so much for leaving the investigation behind. And the question dulled the sparkle she'd had.

"No, can't say that I have. It sounds like a lovely place, though."

"You should visit sometime."

"Maybe I will."

Nathan blew out a breath at the sudden formality of their exchange, like two strangers on the street. Her defenses were firmly raised—she didn't give anything away, unless you looked closely and saw how her eyes changed.

"Anyway, I only ended up with a dual major because I had no idea where I was going. My Dad and Grandad were lawyers, so I felt pressured to go in some kind of similar direction. My real love, though, was psychology, how people react and behave, and why. It ends up the two were pretty complementary, especially when Kevin Mitnick came on the scene, and the whole social-psychological side of hacking became popular. It was always around, as you know—he made it a real phenomenon. I bumped into it at just the right time to write my thesis on it, and the rest was history."

"And you just ended up here?"

"Eventually. Took a few detours first."

He was tired of talking about his life when he had this wonderful woman sitting just a few feet away. He wanted to know more about her, and not as an investigator. This night was fleeting, and he didn't know if there would be another. As the boat turned, starting its slow trajectory back toward shore, the waiter reappeared, delivering espresso and mouthwatering slices of tiramisu. Jennie sat back in her chair as she eyed the dessert.

"I'm so stuffed. This was delicious. It's amazing how the saltwater air will stimulate your appetite."

He knew she was talking about the confection on the table in front of them, yet Nathan felt her words stir a different kind of hunger, tightening every muscle in his body with desire. His appetite was definitely stimulated. *Down, boy,* he commanded himself, striving for control.

Thankfully, Jennie didn't seem to be aware.

"It's such a beautiful night to be out on the water. Thanks for thinking of this."

Abandoning her dessert, she stood, and walked to the rail, looking out over the water. Nathan took his plate and a spoon, joining her. Maybe if his hands and mouth were otherwise occupied, he'd be able to keep them to himself.

He rested against the rail, gazing out over the calm waters of the Bay, dark now as the moon set low in the sky. Looking down he grabbed a chunk of cake with the fork, and lifted it to Jennie's lips. She drew back slightly, shaking her head, but he smiled and wordlessly urged her to indulge. He could barely keep his hand steady as she leaned in and formed her amazing mouth in an O around the end of the fork, slipping the cake into her mouth in such an unconsciously sensual move that he nearly dropped the utensil over the rail.

Instead, he placed it and the plate on a nearby table and reached out, pulling her up against him, glad the "first date" kiss had been gotten out of the way earlier so that he could take his first real kiss now. Taking her lips against his, he slid his hands into that seductive mass of curls, as he'd imagined doing so many times. He sank into the sensual taste of her mixed with the sweet cream and chocolate of the dessert.

Nathan was gratified to feel her hands slide around his waist, her fingers digging into the small of his back. As he felt her nails press against his skin through the thin material of his shirt, his entire body turned into one, long cord of need. Scooping her closer, he deepened the kiss, breathing into her.

Jennie knew she shouldn't be letting it happen, still the moment he'd pulled her in and sealed her mouth in that kiss, she was lost. She'd kissed her share of men, but she'd never been at the mercy of the touch of someone's lips. From the moment Nathan's mouth had captured hers, she could only get closer. Her resistance crumbled, she needed to touch him. He felt *so* good. Solid, warm and completely delicious.

When his deep moan rumbled through her, and she felt every hard, lean part of him aligned with every soft, receptive part of her, she slid her hands down to his backside. She always was a sucker for a nice male butt. As her palms cupped the strong muscles there, she purred against his lips, her fingers unable to resist the urge to explore.

"Jesus, Jennie…" Nathan's breathing was labored against her mouth, his eyes sparkling with wicked promises as he looked down at her, his arms tight around her, inadvertently drawing their pelvises closer together in the process. Suddenly she heard the clinking of dishes and silverware and remembered they weren't alone. Sliding her eyes to the side, she saw the waiter clearing the table, the young man's gaze discreetly looking away from them.

She laughed softly, resting her forehead against his shoulder. "Wow. I completely lost track of where I was…*who* I was…." She laughed again, incredulous at the mind-blanking desire that she'd tumbled into.

"As long as you remembered who *I* was."

The comment was softly spoken against her ear, and she could hear the subtle doubt, the tension, in his voice. She supposed she couldn't blame him— she'd spent so many months putting him off, how could she explain suddenly falling into his arms without so much as a murmur of protest? She was a big girl; she took responsibility for her actions, and she never led guys on. She was very attracted to Nathan; it was why she kept the flowers he sent until the blossoms faded.

Looking up at him, she sighed, framing his face with her hands. He was so damned handsome.

"No, I knew exactly what I was doing, and with whom, Nathan. And I…"

Hope glinted in his eyes. She swallowed the lump in her throat, feeling horrible about all of the deception in her life, and wishing she could just blurt it all out, come clean just once, with this special man. He was so open to her, so ready to take a leap that she didn't know if she could ever take. What was it she'd been about to confess, to admit? Was she ready?

"What, Jennie? You can say it. Remember what I said. No pressure, I promise."

His fingers traced a lazy path along her back, and he stepped back slightly, as if to show her that he was willing to give her room to breathe. The gesture was almost as powerful as a touch, because she knew he meant it. She watched as the docks came into view, their magical trip was almost over. She knew she couldn't tell him the truth about her life; to do so would just endanger his life.

Or maybe she wasn't being so noble, really; the truth was that if she told him everything, he might change his mind about her, and she needed to be with him. At least for tonight, she needed to forget all the reasons she shouldn't do this. She wanted something special, something for *her* that might create a memory she could hold close no matter what the future was. Looking up into his eyes, she took the leap.

"Nathan, I don't kiss a man like we just kissed because I feel pressured into it—I'm way too old for that in case you haven't noticed."

Five years didn't seem like much, but with everything that had happened in her life, she sometimes felt as if she was decades older. Not right now; not with Nathan. He made her feel...young. New. *Happy.*

But shouldn't he want some woman his own age, with no past, no baggage? She held his gaze as the boat slowed. The way he looked at her...she had no doubts that he wanted her, and she was determined to focus on that for now. It was enough.

"I'm glad tomorrow's Saturday," she whispered, leaning in, giving in to the impulse to move her hands over the well-defined muscles of his back. He was slim and strong. A shudder of desire flooded her as she allowed herself to feel things she'd been fighting for a while.

"Why's that?" His voice was husky with desire as he asked the question, her touch affecting him. The knowledge made her smile as she answered.

"So we can sleep in."

She lifted her mouth to his again, and felt him relax and harden all at once, his body hot against hers as he kissed the breath from her all the way back to the pier. She hadn't met any men her own age or older who could kiss half as well. She preferred to think he'd come by the talent naturally, rather than having had too much practice.

By the time the boat docked, they were both overcome with the need to find somewhere private, and Nathan hastily squared things with the waiter and took Jennie's hand, hurrying her gently from the boat and back to his car.

Once inside the sleek little Mustang, they combated the small space over the gearshift, all over each other again until laughingly, they parted, but never stopped touching completely as Nathan raced back to Jennie's apartment. She smiled, anticipation buzzing through her in a way she hadn't experienced in a long time.

Appreciation welled with desire as he pulled up into a parking spot in front of her building and cut the engine. He was willing to come to her place, to go where she felt familiar and comfortable. She had a feeling she'd only discovered the tip of the iceberg when it came to finding out how special Nathan Reilly really was.

3

IMAGES OF THEM FALLING in the door and tearing at each other's clothes raced through Nathan's brain as he tried to keep to the speed limit, but Jennie's hand tracing erotic messages on his upper thigh made it hard to hold back. He needed out of this car, and out of his clothes, *soon.*

After the frantic rush to the apartment, as soon as they stepped inside the door, breathless and laughing, everything slowed down. They stood, facing each other, saying nothing, and he crossed, taking her hands in his.

"You're sure?"

"Yes."

The simple response was all he needed. With a gentle tug she was in his arms again, and the passion lit even more brightly than before. Now that they were alone, now that Nathan was where he'd dreamed of being for months on end, he found he didn't want to rush, as urgent as the need was.

He'd always preferred hard, fast sex, reveling in the urgency and the energy of the act, yet there was something about Jennie that made him hold back and savor every move, each touch. It was a new kind of intensity, born of waiting so long for her, he supposed. He slipped a finger beneath the shoulder of her soft sweater, sliding it under the bra strap, and eased it down, smoothing the tender skin of her shoulder. She was so soft.

Leaning in, he buried his face in her neck and inhaled her scent, then darted his tongue out for a taste, loving the way her head fell back and how she seemed to purr as he nuzzled her, investigating all those secret spots he'd wondered about for so long. The hidden silk behind her ear. The visible pulse at the base of her throat that hammered as he lifted his other hand to her waist, sliding it up and down her spine, causing her to bow her body into his, issuing an erotic invitation when she pressed against him just so. They fit perfectly, as if they were made to be this way. The idea moved him profoundly.

When she began her own exploration, yanking his shirt free and sliding over the skin of his lower back and then up, he momentarily closed his eyes, reminding himself he wanted to go slow, though his body was starting to disagree with that plan. Her seductive touch, still somewhat tentative, as if she hadn't quite made up her mind, convinced him that slow was the right choice.

The bulge in Nathan's pants that nestled so sweetly against her abdomen made Jennie's imagination spike with images of driving him over the edge. A part of her held back, still feeling, for the first time in a long time, like a liar. It didn't seem to matter that the lies were to protect herself, to protect others. Would he still be here if he knew the secrets she kept?

Now wasn't the moment to worry about it. She felt more aroused than she ever had, and yet her worries were not quite quenched.

"Jennie, you can change your mind if you want. I don't want you doing anything you don't want to," Nathan said. His breathing was labored and she smiled, lifting her hand to slide the pad of her fingers over the fine film of sweat that had formed on his brow.

Nathan had some serious self-control, another plus, in her book. But she wanted him to go wild with her. And she knew just how to make him do it.

"I don't want to stop, Nathan. It's just that I didn't expect this. I didn't expect to feel so much so fast and, well, I'm a little worried about the fact that we work together. Sex complicates things."

That much was true, she thought, though it was becoming less and less important as he touched her in all the right places.

"Let's not think about work tonight."

She nodded, agreeing, glad at least to be able to tell the truth to him about some things, "It's also been a while for me."

"Then we need to make this extra special, don't we?"

"I don't think that's going to be a problem. It feels pretty special to me already."

She could have kicked herself for her impulsive response as an answering flicker of passion, and some deeper emotion, passed over his expression. She couldn't lead him along, she cautioned herself; she didn't know how much she could give to him. Though the crazy thudding of her heart was urging her to give him everything. She'd wanted something special, right? Something more? Well, this was it.

Nathan was special, she could feel it in her bones, and not being a woman of half measures or tepid emotions, she couldn't deny her response to him. Permitting this to mean more than just sex was a risk. Her entire life was about risk, so what was she waiting for?

"Where's your bedroom?" His question was posed on a hushed breath, but she had other ideas. She wanted to let him know she was in this, one hundred percent.

"I want you now, Nate. Here."

The comment was filled with such sexy promise he didn't argue, but dived in to obey her command with a gusto that nearly dropped her to her knees as he kissed her with the full force of masculine desire, holding nothing back. She answered him with equal fervor, and they moved across the small living room toward the sofa.

When his hands slipped up underneath her sweater and massaged her nipples, tweaking and pinching the tender nubs, she wondered if she would even make it to the couch. She gasped as her body coiled inside at the sharp sensations his touch created, feeling a spill of release quickly approaching.

"You're amazing…so beautiful…so responsive…"

His encouragement wiped out the last of any doubts she had as she let go completely, winding her hands through his hair and urging him downward. Happy to comply, he shoved the sweater up over her head and brought his hot, searching mouth to her breasts. It took only moments before she cried out, coming hard as he sucked, arching into him as ripples of pleasure racked through her. When he raised his head, lifting a hand to push some hair from her brow, his hand was shaking.

"Holy shit, Jen. I can't believe you came like that…."

"I'm so—"

He shook his head vigorously, his skin ruddy with desire.

"It was so hot…can you do it again?"

Jennie smiled at the wonderful question, her body turning liquid under his mouth and hands as he applied his mouth to her skin again, searching out every tender, excruciatingly sensitive spot. Where had he learned to be so thorough with a woman's body?

"I can almost guarantee it," she answered, giving herself over and forgetting everything but the way he made her feel.

"UNDRESS ME, JEN."

"With pleasure."

The two simple words rocked him to the core; he could get off on her voice alone, he thought, still reeling that just his touch and his kiss had pushed *her* over the edge. It was daunting, the fire between them hotter than anything he imagined, and anything he'd ever experienced before. He was ready for more. He wanted it all.

Somehow she'd managed to undo all the buttons while he kissed her. He couldn't stay away from her, even just for the few moments it took for her to peel his clothes off, and to shed the rest of hers. That final act of confirming she wanted this as much as he did, of committing to the moment, moved him even more than her strong physical response had.

She peeled the shirt from him, dipping to suck on one dark nipple, enchanted with his chest and running her fingers over the light sprinkling of chest hair. His cock twitched impatiently, hungry for those caresses and kisses to cover him there, too. But he had to stop her before he lost it and completely embarrassed himself.

Within moments, they were both completely bare; facing each other in the warm light of the room, taking in the sight of each other's bodies. She was even lovelier than he could have ever imagined. Curved and full, she was beautifully formed, her skin a satin olive tone that bespoke her Italian heritage, the dark triangle of silken hair at the V of her legs thick and soft and tempting him to touch, to taste. The dusky areolae of her nipples accentuated perfectly rounded breasts with velvet brown tips that had been heaven to taste.

"You're amazing," she said as she stepped forward, breathing the words into his mouth, pressing the cleft of her moist sex next to his painfully hard shaft. He drew back, looking up into her face.

"I was just thinking the same about you." He couldn't take his eyes from her as he responded, trying to cover all of the bases before the inevitable progressed. "Anything else we should get out in the open before this happens?"

"No. I'm good. On the pill, and no problems to speak of. You?"

"I was tested during my physical when I joined the team, and haven't been with anyone since."

She looked amazed at what he'd just revealed. "You haven't slept with anyone since you joined HotWires?"

He lifted his hand, brushing the backs of his fingers along her cheek. "Well, at first I had the move and settling into the job, the new city. And then I saw you. I didn't want anyone after that."

Her eyes turned molten, telling him how affected she was by his confession, and he was glad it hadn't scared her off. It was true—one morning he'd seen her laughing with Sarah over coffee. The sun had been shining through the window behind her, and her expression had been lit with amusement at whatever story Sarah had been telling.

He'd been rooted to the spot, watching, reminded of something his dad had told him about a similar moment when he'd met Nate's mother. About his *grá mo chroí,* or the love of his heart.

Though he'd noticed her right away when he joined the team—she was a beautiful woman—he hadn't been looking for a relationship. He was all about work, and it was clear she wasn't interested in getting involved with anyone. Nevertheless from that moment on, seeing her standing there in the sun, Nathan hadn't wanted another woman. Afterward, he'd started sending her flowers, and stopping by her desk just to tell her jokes to see her face light up with that smile. He wanted to make her smile almost more than he wanted to breathe.

The mood shifted, and she looked up at him, open and vulnerable. Conflict suddenly twisted with passion in his gut—how could he see this through when he was keeping some major secrets? How could he make her trust him when he was investigating her, looking into her life to see if she was a criminal, a traitor to his friends?

Because he didn't believe it. He had good instincts, and there was no way he could feel this way about someone who was dirty. Ian and EJ were smart, thorough. They would never have taken her on if she was less than what they believed her to be. He was going to prove she was a victim here, innocent.

The thought soothed his guilty conscience as she apparently was tired of waiting and lifted up, gently pressing her lips to his, her breasts caressing his chest while she explored his mouth in an intimate yet demanding response. She wanted him; he wanted her. At the moment, it was that simple.

Lowering slowly, he lay back on the sofa, pulling her down on top, having her set the pace, control their loving—this time. She took him inside while their mouths still mated, easily and without hesitation, and his low rumble of excitement filled her as she sheathed him completely, rotating her hips slowly and encouraging him with her own moans as he gripped her backside tightly, helping her move.

"Jennie, you're so warm inside, so soft…."

She gasped, holding on as he lunged beneath her. Not one to stay passive, he gripped her hips firmly, helping her ride him harder as she wove her hands into his hair, kissing him deeply as they both began shuddering with release. Gasping in ecstasy, he drove inside of her, losing every final bit of control, and loving every second.

"WHAT DO YOU WANT for breakfast?"

"You."

Jennie rolled over, and nipped his shoulder playfully. It had been one of the best nights of her life, and it was the weekend. She'd never awakened in bed with a man and just lounged, wondering what the day had to offer—if he would want to spend the day, and maybe another night—with her. No, the usual protocol was up, shower, a kiss in thanks and out. However, not this time; not with Nathan.

She found herself suddenly a little wary—would he want to leave? Would it be too much if he knew how much she wanted him to stay? Too clingy? Too fast?

Her hand caressed his chest. Working lower, she curled her fingers around his stiff cock and elicited a groan, a good sign he wasn't in a hurry to leave.

They'd made love several times throughout the night, and he'd always managed to make sure that she'd remained in control in one way or another.

Or maybe he was just a guy who enjoyed a woman being in control; the notion surprised her. In fact, her mind started to race with all the delightful possibilities being the dominant sexual partner presented. Her imagination took flight as she continued stroking and caressing him. Surprisingly, he reached down, stilling her hand.

"How about breakfast?" he asked again, smiling, his voice uneven—she'd obviously been having an effect. She pulled back, relenting.

"You're really hungry, huh? For food?"

"You've given me quite a workout. Do you have anything here, or do you want to go out?"

Flustered by his apparent rejection, she tried to

play it cool and sat up, making sure he couldn't see her face in the meantime, just in case her expression gave too much away.

"I have some stuff in the kitchen."

As she started to get up, he grabbed her wrist and pulled her back, kissing her soundly.

"I'll go. You relax."

"But—"

"I'll cook. You save your strength. You're going to need it." His smile was promising, his erection still full. She warmed, hating how relieved she felt.

"Maybe I'll take a shower then."

"You go ahead. If I finish soon enough, I'll join you."

Nathan winked and stood up, watching her with a smile. It would have been so easy to give in, but he really was hungry. And if truth be told, he needed a moment. The events of the night before had been powerful, socking a punch to his emotions that he'd never felt before, and he'd awoken knowing he was in a serious bind.

Heading into the living room where his pants lay crumpled on the floor, he put them on, not bothering with his shirt. He bent over, picking up a withered blossom that had fallen from a vase of flowers, lifting it to his nose and still detecting the sweet scent. He thought about bringing flowers to bed, and rubbing that scent all over Jen's skin. His cock twitched at the thought and he sighed—he was a goner.

Memories from last night assaulted him, followed by a wave of disgust at what he knew he had to do—and this was the perfect opportunity. He heard the shower come on, and took a deep breath, his smile fading. It was too easy to forget about what he'd learned, too tempting to just set it aside and refuse to do the department's dirty work. A twist of shame knotted in his chest—he cared about her, nevertheless he had a job to do. What a shitty wall to be backed up against.

If what they said was true, then Jennie's—Maria's—existence could be a threat to all of their lives, no matter how impossible that seemed. And if by investigating her possible guilt he could prove she was innocent…that idea alone motivated him to move forward, his heart pounding.

He whispered her real name, closing his eyes and feeling the sound of it cross his lips. He'd always liked her as Jennie, but last night, she'd been Maria—dark, exotic, stunning.

He stood, peeking around the doorway to reassure himself that she was still in the shower, and walked to her dressers, lifting the tops of the small, decorative jewelry boxes, checking the bottom for hidden compartments and doing the same in her drawers and closet.

Moving swiftly and efficiently, he made his way back out to her desk, checked the drawers, her desktop, under the blotter—and found her password scrawled on the back of a restaurant receipt, buried in a sentence reminding her to make reservations next time.

It was clever—anyone else looking wouldn't have any idea, thinking it was just a note on the back of a receipt, but Nathan spotted the acronym that formed with the first letter of each word, and added in the amount of the bill at the end—presto. He turned on her computer—the password worked, and he quickly shut it down. No time for that now.

Poking around a bit more, he found nothing else. Had he really expected to? Jennie wasn't stupid; she wouldn't leave evidence lying around. A thorough search through her computer files might expose something more. Still, he couldn't repress his relief that at least so far, he'd found absolutely nothing to substantiate the claims against her.

He heard the water shut off and hurried into the kitchen, whipping open the refrigerator door and in the process nearly sending the items inside flying out.

Luckily, he was swiftly able to throw an assortment of foods on the table—fruit, cheese, jam, some bagels and half of a grocery-store Danish she had left. He found the coffee on the counter, started a pot. He could hear Jennie shuffling around in the bedroom, drawers opening and closing. A few minutes later she walked into the kitchen, fresh in her white satin robe.

"This looks wonderful—thank you."

"Let me get the coffee—it's almost done. Black, right?"

She looked up, her gaze curious. "How did you know that?"

"It's how you took your espresso last night. And I've seen you drink black coffee at the office, remember?"

She shook her head, and laughed. He'd have to be careful. She was always "on"—it was a hazard of the job.

"I'm not used to anyone noticing things like that. Or being so sweet."

"I'm sorry I didn't have time to cook anything." He meant that more than she could know.

"This is great. I don't always eat breakfast. Much of the stuff I buy goes to waste, so it's nice to share it with someone."

They sat, and suddenly the easy banter disappeared, and things felt a little awkward. Nathan wasn't sure what changed. They silently ate their breakfast. Finally, Jennie's shoulders sagged, and a sigh escaped her lips.

"What's wrong, Jen?"

"Nothing…I don't know. It's been amazing, last night, now, sitting here with you, but—"

"Too much too fast?"

"I don't know. I like being with you. I want this, but I'm not sure I can promise you anything more than this, Nathan. And we should make that clear before things get any more…involved."

"Why? Are you secretly married? A CIA spy or something?"

She smiled, but it didn't reach her eyes. Had he stumbled too close to the truth?

"No, nothing that dramatic. I never planned on getting seriously involved with anyone, and that hasn't changed."

"Not yet."

"Nathan—"

"Jen."

He stood, crossing to her side of the table, kneeling by her chair. She was the most beautiful woman he'd ever seen. Ever been with. He almost didn't care if she was a criminal. He reached up, rubbing a bit of jam from her lip with the pad of his thumb, and was delighted when he saw the flare of desire in her eyes from the touch.

"Let's just go with it, okay? See what happens. We have something special, I think, and we should explore it."

"I don't want to make promises, Nathan."

"The only thing I'm asking for is that you'll spend time with me, enjoy this thing we have, and be willing to see what happens. Is that too much?"

He moved closer, caressing her mouth with his, nuzzling his cheek to hers. Her hands had fallen to her lap, her fingers wrapped around each other, tense. Was she just nervous because of her secret life in the program or was she hiding more than that?

For now, he put those questions aside. He'd find out soon enough, one way or the other. At the moment, he just needed to kiss her again. She tasted like mint toothpaste, raspberry jam and butter, and though he hadn't eaten much, it was the best breakfast he'd ever had.

The stalwart resolve that Jennie had always managed to maintain was melting under Nathan's lips and caresses, and so was she. It was pathetic. And wonderful. Had she allowed herself to feel this much in years? Ever? Forgetting breakfast, she wound her arms around his neck, sinking into the kiss. He was right, perhaps—just enjoy it and see what happened.

She'd had a few affairs, but no real romances—was it wrong, just this once, to reach out for what she longed for? Had her paranoia and fear gotten the best of her? Living the way she had, in hiding, meant that her uncle won. He'd taken so much of her life away. Not anymore.

Spurred on by her thoughts, she sank from her chair to the floor with Nathan.

"We seem to end up on the floor a lot," he teased.

"Do you mind?"

"Not in the least. I want you to do something."

"What?"

Without a word, he snaked his hand behind her back, and in one deft move, had her lying on the polished hardwood floor before she knew it. They'd had the same physical training, apparently he was much more accomplished at it than she was.

"No fair! I didn't see that coming."

He smiled down at her with seduction and mischief in his eyes.

"All's fair, my sweet." He wiggled his eyebrows comically, making her laugh. "I want you to stay there. Just lie still, and let me take care of you."

"But I want—"

"Trust me to give you what you want, Jen—and what I want, as well. I think they're probably one and the same."

She doubted that, then took a breath, willing to play along. His hands slid up the insides of her thighs, spreading her to his view. So he didn't just want her to be dominant all the time. Thank God, because as much as she had enjoyed being in the driver's seat, having him take control was so exciting she actually trembled as he pushed the robe aside and murmured something appreciative about her not bothering with underwear after her shower.

She felt a little odd as he continued to gaze at her so intimately; she was exposed, and vulnerable beneath his gaze.

"Nathan…"

He dipped down, laying a tender kiss on the inside of her thigh, and cut her commentary short. All she could do was sigh. Then moan. Then cry out, as his fingers traveled upward, finding their mark between her legs and stroking her intimately as he left hot licks everywhere, but not in the place she most wanted them.

"Nathan, please."

"Uh-uh. I'm in charge this time, sweetheart. I'm setting the pace."

"Don't worry, I'm more than ready."

"I'm not." He grinned down at her, and she peered at the erection tenting the front of his pants.

"You look pretty ready to me."

"Just be a good girl and hush."

She raised an eyebrow—he was telling her to hush? And she felt like anything but a good girl, spread out on her own kitchen floor like a buffet. Her eyes widened when he reached up on the table. She saw him take the jam jar and stick a finger in.

His intentions were no longer a mystery as he fingered a dollop of jam between her legs; she closed her eyes, waiting for what was next.

"You're wicked."

She barely managed the words as he spread more of the preserve over her and set the jam back on the table. When she opened her eyes and saw he'd undressed, his fully aroused naked body towering over her, she almost—almost—swooned. His voice was husky and full of promise as he knelt again, slouching down between her sprawled legs.

"And you're delicious."

He began licking that jam from her skin, diving his tongue between the plump lips of her sex, reaching to eat every bit of raspberry he'd covered her with and throwing her into cataclysmic pleasure in the process.

She tried to wrap her legs around him, but he pushed her thighs farther apart with his forearms. As it turned out, that worked, too—very, very well.

His hands and mouth were everywhere, and by the third orgasm, she felt a tear slide down her temple to the floor, and she begged him to take her, another first.

This time he listened, rising up and placing her legs, weak from straining against his hold, securely around his hips. She lifted, and he thrust to the hilt.

She felt like a wild animal, crazed and writhing, sinking her nails into his back as they moved together in a furious rhythm unlike anything else she'd ever experienced. She didn't hold back, and neither did he, penetrating her deeply, stroking her very soul until she clenched around him, coming again, her body feeling tense and slack and hot all at once. She didn't think she could go on, but he held her, pumping into her with increased speed and need, in a way that thrilled her.

She moaned encouragement, needing to connect with him on every basic level, delighted to tell him what she wanted in the coarsest of terms when she discovered that dirty talk—*really* dirty talk—drove him wild.

She watched him rear back, beautiful as his chest heaved, and he drove into her one final time, spilling seed inside of her, his own hoarse cries mingling with hers. Then he collapsed on the floor by her side, panting hard.

"It seems to get more amazing each time," she whispered, feeling worn-out, as if she could sleep where she lay. He pulled her up onto his shoulder, so she would be more comfortable and her eyelids drooped. She smiled against his chest as he kissed her hair. As consciousness dimmed, she felt more than sated. More than desired. She'd experienced those things before. But this time, with Nathan, she'd felt...*consumed. Cherished.*

Another first.

4

"SO WHO'S THE *JAMOOK?*" Bruno looked out over the golf course, not paying much attention to the picture of the young man that Tony was holding out in front of him.

"Nathan Reilly. The FBI guys we leaked the information about Maria to contacted the Norfolk Police, Internal Affairs, specifically. They went directly to this guy."

"What does this have to do with Maria?"

"Not sure yet."

Bruno lost sight of his shot, straightening. "Internal Affairs? What's their business in this?"

Tony shuffled, looking across the links, distinctly uncomfortable. "Well, we only know she went into the Witness Protection program. We don't know what she does for a living. There's a chance she works in a police department. Maybe she's even a cop."

Bruno shook his head in disbelief. "How the hell could she become a cop? Is that even legal?"

"It's not like she's an ex-con, Uncle. She never committed any crime—"

"Against her family, she did."

"Not legally. I suppose she could go or do anything she wanted. If IA is involved, it stands to reason she's involved as a cop."

"What the hell is this world coming to?"

Tony shrugged. "I suppose they'd be happy to have her, with what she knows. It should make our job easier."

"How d'ya figure?"

"If he is involved, we follow him, we follow the IA guys, we find her."

Bruno shook his head again. "Almost too easy." Personally, he liked a challenge. Like hitting this tiny ball a couple of hundred feet into that tiny hole.

Still, a member of his family—and a female member, at that—a cop? The idea gave him *agita*.

"It's not like the old days, when the Feds provided us some challenge. Real men, back then. Wished some of them were on our side." He pulled back, followed through, watching the shot and feeling satisfied enough with where it landed. "You got him bugged?"

"Not yet."

"Well, what the hell you waiting for?"

"It's not an easy thing, to get a bead on a cop."

"A bead?"

"You know, a tracking device. A bug."

"Why do you call it a bead?"

Tony shrugged. "They're small. They look like beads. I heard it on TV or somethin'."

"Just say what you mean. I can't figure out half of what you young guys are talking about anymore."

"Sorry."

"I don't care how hard it is, get it done. Bug all of 'em, the IA guys, the computer guy and anyone else we have to. We must have someone down there we can slip a little extra to, make it worth their while?"

"I'll find someone."

"You do that."

"I'M TELLING YOU, your lead stinks. There's nothing going on."

Nathan sat at the coffee shop table, trying to get his point across to the very unreceptive men sitting across from him. Suits. God, they drove him nuts. No wonder no one liked IA—had they forgotten how to be cops? Or what it was like to be a cop?

"It's been five days since you started your investigation. You can't possibly draw any conclusions yet." Detective Norris's tone was dismissive, and Nathan shifted forward, feeling edgy. Feeling like pushing back. If the older detective thought he was dominating some rookie, green behind the ears and willing to just go along without a peep, he had another think coming. Nathan didn't like the man, he didn't like the job and he didn't like being dismissed.

"I told you. I talked with her, I searched her home, I got her computer password and poured through all of her files last night, and there's nothing. Zip. Nothing there. Don't you get that?"

Something flickered in the eyes of the older man who sat across from him, but other than that, the officers kept their tone steady. They'd obviously been down this road before, but not with him. Norris appeared unmoved and just kept his questions coming. Nathan sat back in disgust.

"How'd you manage to get inside so quickly?"

It took a lot for Nathan not to drop his eyes, not to give too much away. The last thing he needed was for Norris to find out the truth about his relationship with Jennie.

"We're friends. We work in the same unit. It wasn't hard to get an invite over for dinner."

"That's all?"

"Yeah, that's all."

"So you're not sleeping with her? I mean, she is a sexy woman." He laughed, and it wasn't a nice laugh. "Those legs alone, hoo-ah! And being in close quarters…I almost couldn't blame you if you got the opportunity, kid. Almost."

Nathan remained cool. He had to. But later, after he proved Jennie was innocent, Norris would be seeing him again, he promised himself. For a very unofficial visit. For Jennie's sake, he had to play along, distasteful as it was to be discussing her like this. He'd just shared five fantastic days with her— they could barely keep their hands off of each other—and now he was here listening to Norris talk about her as if she was some kind of bimbo. Nathan channeled his fury into sarcasm.

"Sounds to me like *you* want to date her, Norris. But I guess at your age, well, you don't stand a chance with a babe like that, do you? Maybe that's why you're so nasty all the time—not getting any?"

Nathan's voice was just cutting enough to be believable. He hoped. The men laughed, and Nathan curled his fists under the table.

"Wouldn't throw her out of bed, that's true."

Nathan had to change the conversation before he lost it and pummeled Norris into a pulp.

"I still don't get why you didn't go through Ian or EJ for this."

"They know her—go way back, and they could be in on it," Norris persisted, though he sounded as though he had doubts on that score. "At the very least, they would be blind to her faults, unwilling to believe the worst of her, no matter what's right in front of their faces. EJ was involved with her once—it clouds the issues."

"You're writing a big check with your mouth that your ass had better be able to cash."

"Cool down, kid. We know all about Arthur and Lancelot and the Camelot you guys have up there on the fourth floor. Heaven forbid anyone say anything about the HotWires. But no one is above the law, and if we find out they're covering for her—"

"So basically, as far as Ian and EJ go, you've got nothing. And really, you don't have anything on Jennie yet, either."

"They're not being investigated—yet. It depends on what you find. But they can't know. You breathe a word of this and—"

"I won't. I wouldn't want anyone to know I've been shanghaied by you jerks."

Nathan was telling the absolute truth about that. If anyone knew he was working against his own team, his career was shot. None of the cops around him would want anything to do with him. If Jennie was innocent, all of this would just go away, and no one would ever know. The whole deal made him feel dirty. Worse.

"You just do your job, Reilly. And do it right."

"I don't know what else I could possibly look for. I told you I didn't find anything."

"You wait, you stay close. There's no rush. She's been in this too long, and she's too smart to leave evidence lying around. It's not surprising you didn't find anything sitting on her kitchen table."

Norris took something out of his jacket. "Here's a disc, kid." He used the term in such a condescending way Nathan felt a new riff of anger, but he maintained control…barely.

"…names and pictures of contacts she might seek out or be in contact with. You just keep an eye out if she decides to go for a walk on the beach, if she so much as makes casual conversation with someone on the street. If you recognize one of the people on this disc, we want to know."

Nathan took the disc and slid it in his jacket, too pissed to say another word.

"You said this woman's your friend—but if you hold back on this, if you protect her, we'll send someone else in who won't, and you'll both take the hit. Even if it feels like shit, remember you're working on the right side." Norris's voice had modulated a bit.

"Gee, thanks for the pep talk." Nathan glared at the two men who stood and strode out of the shop. He watched Norris and his partner get into the SUV and drive away. "And you can bet I won't hold back," he promised under his breath.

JENNIE EXITED the ladies' room and hopped down the hall on one foot, trying to get her other shoe on and balance at the same time. She was late. Nathan was supposed to pick her up at six, and it was ten after. He was probably downstairs waiting, and she didn't want him to have to come back up to get her. They'd agreed to meet for dinner again—they'd barely been out of each other's sight since the previous Friday night.

Still, they were trying to keep up a façade at work, keeping their budding relationship to themselves. Partly because it was more fun that way, but also because, well…just because.

The shoe didn't quite make it on as she stumbled in surprise, almost falling against the wall, and would have if a strong set of arms didn't interrupt her fall. She looked up into Nathan's amused eyes as he steadied her.

Jennie smiled, disengaging long enough to step forward, seeking her other shoe, and putting it on.

"Nathan! I'm so sorry you had to come way back up here for me. I was just on my way down."

"My pleasure," he drawled, sending shivers down her spine.

Jennie, with both shoes safely on, smoothed her hair, and smiled at Nathan, slipping her arms around his neck. "So where are we going for dinner? I'm starving…"

He was oddly stiff in her arms, even as he stepped in for her hug, and planted a quick, chaste kiss on her cheek before he moved back, out of her embrace. She dropped her arms, frowning.

"Okay. What's wrong?"

"Someone could see us."

She scoped out the hall; they were alone. Sure they were trying to keep things private, but there was no need for paranoia. Everyone was gone for the day, more or less, and they were consenting adults. There were no professional rules keeping them from being in a relationship. He was so clearly uncomfortable with her closeness that she relented, not wanting to exacerbate the problem. Yet she couldn't help feeling slightly hurt and unsure what to say. So she said nothing, but her uneasiness must have been obvious since he placed a hand on her arm—a *friendly* hand—though his voice was low and intimate as he spoke.

"Jen, I'm sorry, I just want to keep this between us for the moment. I thought you agreed?"

She blinked, shocked to find her eyes stinging at his mild rejection, and astounded to be moved to tears by a guy she'd been seeing for barely a week. She moved away from his touch, still feeling stung. She did want to keep their affair private, however, that didn't mean she was ashamed to be seen with him in public.

Or maybe, on some unconscious level, she wanted others to know. Maybe having others know would make what was happening feel even more…real. The discovery shocked her. She'd known she felt something for Nathan, but she was startled by the realization that she'd built so many hopes around him already.

That was clearly a mistake; Nathan obviously didn't feel the same way. She tried to sound normal as she responded.

"I do. You're right. Maybe we should just skip dinner tonight, you know, and give ourselves some space, because, you know, God forbid we could be seen out at a restaurant or in the parking lot together or…"

Her Italian blood had given her a strong temper, and when it was wrapped up with so many other passionate emotions, she felt completely tipped out of kilter. So much for acting normal.

"Jen, c'mon…."

She shook her head, stalking off in the other direction. She didn't need this. She didn't need *him*.

As she stumbled again, her shoe not quite on tightly enough, she swore hotly, blinking back those damned, stupid tears that kept blurring her vision. She was determined not to make *that* big of a fool out of herself.

Nathan solved the problem by grabbing her wrist and pulling her in close to him. Her furious eyes met his as her chest heaved with temper, her skin flushed, her lips narrowed as she spat words at him.

"I thought you didn't want to be this close to me in public."

"I changed my mind. Let's live dangerously."

He didn't give her another chance to object, pinning both wrists behind her back and kissing her senseless, enjoying the way she struggled to escape his grasp, even as she kissed him back.

"Keep moving like that and we're going to end up down on the floor, honey."

"That would just be awkward for everyone."

Both of their heads whipped around to see Sarah standing by the HotWires' office door, smirking. Nathan rolled his eyes, but didn't let go of Jennie, who struggled even more now that they'd been caught.

"Don't you ever go home?"

Sarah just laughed at the clear frustration in his

question, and waved behind her as she turned in the opposite direction, heading out.

"Get a room, Nate."

Nathan looked down at Jennie, whose anger had been transformed into concern, he could tell, as she guardedly watched Sarah walk down the hallway.

Nathan felt like an ass—coming from the meeting with IA, all he could imagine was Norris or one of his flunkies following him through the door and seeing him with Jennie. He thought he could convince her that they couldn't be public with their affair for professional reasons—which was partly true, because if they were caught, they were both in hot water with IA. But he hadn't wanted to hurt her. He never wanted to hurt her. He tipped his forehead against hers.

"I'm sorry for being an ass. I guess I just thought you wanted to keep things under wraps more. You never seemed to like it when I flirted with you in the office."

"I didn't…I mean, I did—"

"Never mind. I wasn't thinking."

Jennie looked at him from under the thick veil of lashes, spiked with tears. "Apology accepted."

He stepped closer, kissing those tears away, cursing himself for causing her even a moment's pain.

"I guess I should take you somewhere fancy for dinner to make up for it?"

She smiled, lifting a hand to his face. "Anywhere will do. I'm just glad to see you."

"It's only been about three hours that we've been apart."

"And your point is?"

His heart leaped in a very dangerous way as her emotions filled her eyes. Did she even know how much she was showing him about how she felt? Even when she lost her temper, which made her more gorgeous than ever, she was showing him how much she was coming to care. Could she know how badly he wanted to tell her how he felt the same way?

That couldn't happen; not yet.

She reached up to kiss him again, and he groaned, pulling himself away, teasing her playfully.

"I'm serious—you keep doing that, and right here on the floor, lady…."

"Okay. I guess we should go get dinner then."

"Is something fast okay, so we can get home and get to the good stuff?" His voice was hopeful.

"You read my mind," she whispered next to his ear.

THEY ENDED UP AT HIS PLACE, which was perfectly fine with Jennie. She'd been curious, honestly, to see where he lived, hoping it wouldn't be some twenty-something bachelor pad with cans of Chef Boyardee in the kitchen along with paper plates, beer and some other woman's panties hanging over a chair. Even if it was, she wanted this peek into his life, to see who he was. She appreciated that he hadn't minded coming to her place over the last few nights.

She was pleasantly surprised. The apartment didn't have a lot of furniture; what he had, though, was of good quality and taste. Modern, square, masculine lines worked well with the bold colors, and he even had some decent artwork displayed.

His tenth-floor apartment looked down over the Elizabeth River and the Norfolk waterfront. There was a small balcony. When he invited her to see the view, she demurred, a fear of heights plaguing her from childhood.

She walked around some more while he chose a wine from his small collection, which she could tell he was very proud of. Investigating the rooms, she found herself particularly drawn to a few beautiful Celtic rugs and tapestries that adorned the hardwood floors and hung on the walls.

"Your place is beautiful. I love this rug—is the pattern symbolic?"

"Mmm, hmm." He handed her a glass of red wine, and held his up to the light, inspecting it, apparently lost in thought. "I've been saving this. Braida's Bricco del' Uccellone, 1999. A little pricey for my budget, still I couldn't resist."

She regarded him curiously. "Where does an Irish guy from Beantown learn to speak Italian that smoothly? Did you spend time in Europe?"

He nodded, sniffing the wine and swirling it in his glass, not answering her question right away. She could wait. Jennie was intrigued by this side of him, and glad to discover it. There was definitely more to Nathan than met the eye, though she couldn't take her eyes off of him. He moved with such easy, masculine grace, she couldn't get enough of watching him. She would have said he was too young to be this sophisticated, but she'd have been wrong. He'd surprised her in every way, and that was making him more and more irresistible.

"I traveled for about a year before I joined the team. I was doing some international consulting, and I considered living there. The technology and technological issues in Europe and Africa are interesting and they're way ahead of us here."

"Really? I didn't know that."

He nodded, sipping his wine thoughtfully. "I did some freelance consulting there and learned a lot. Their wireless technology challenges are astounding—some areas are completely wireless, and they are even functioning completely via cell phone technology. Your cell is your credit card, debit card, one little individual resource center."

"And your expertise in security was probably attractive to them because of that. I imagine the privacy concerns are huge."

"They are, and there are some very established computer crime teams, as well. I visited my relatives in Ireland, got in touch with my roots and the world around me. I thought seriously about staying. In the end, I missed my family here. My Dad got sick and that brought me home faster than I expected. Once I was back, I heard about the team, and gave Ian a call. The rest is history."

"Do you wish you'd gone back?"

"I did at first. I loved it there, but my family needed me here, and then Ian made me an offer I couldn't refuse." His gaze locked onto hers. "And then there was you."

He tipped his glass to hers before sipping, savoring the moment. Jennie had never experienced a raised heartbeat just watching a man drink some wine, but she did now. His eyes were lit with erotic promise, then he turned away and gestured to the other side of the room.

"That rug you were admiring was a gift from a cousin on my mother's side. This one was even more special since it came directly from her home."

"And you said the pattern is symbolic? It's a snake?"

"Yes. It's a symbol of new beginnings. My cousin received it as a housewarming present when she moved into her new home, and she wanted me to have it, since I was in one of those 'in between' places in life. You know, having left behind where I was, not sure what was coming next, just sort of wandering. The snake represents power, rebirth and new beginnings. It's a very common symbol in Celtic designs."

"I see—when a snake sheds its skin, it's a new beginning."

"Exactly. The old Celts believed in reincarnation—continuous rebirth until complete spiritual fulfillment is achieved. The symbol is also an expression of the difficulties our ancestors survived, the idea that every day is a new beginning—even difficult times will pass."

"How wonderful to have something so beautiful that reminds you every time you look at it of your family."

A pang of wistfulness suddenly overcame her. She remembered a lovely Italian watch that had been passed down from the old country, from family to family. It would have never been hers—when her father died, it would have gone to Tony, her younger brother. She'd always admired it, and there were other heirlooms in her home, lace tablecloths, imported glass vases and candlesticks. Her mother always recounted the history of each piece when it was used, keeping the memories of who had owned them before alive. She felt the loss of that past very deeply. It was a sense of emptiness that she kept at bay most of the time.

"Are you okay?"

Nathan's concerned question shook her out of her reverie, and she almost tipped her wine.

"I'm sorry. I was thinking about my family for a moment."

"I imagine you miss them."

She had to pause, doing a second take before she realized he meant that she must miss her "adopted family" because they were dead. The wine was fuzzing her thoughts; for a second, she'd felt as though he was seeing right through her to the truth.

"I do. Time passes and wounds heal, but sometimes I miss them horribly." That much was true, and she felt better just to be able to share it with someone, even if he didn't know the whole truth.

"Do you have things that were theirs?"

She shook her head, hating every minute that she had to keep her lie alive. "No, they…didn't have much."

"I'm sorry. I didn't mean to make you sad."

"I'm not. How could I be sad? Here with you?"

She smiled, chasing away the past by looking into Nathan's eyes, so full of desire for her. She sipped the wine, focusing on the warmth of it on her tongue.

"This is great—not too tannic. A fine vintage." She laughed a little. "Just like me."

He smiled softly. "I wondered if that issue was going to come up again."

"What's that?"

"The difference in our ages."

"Five years. Your twenty-eight to my thirty-three. I was riding my bike when you were just being pushed into the world. I'd graduated college when you were a senior in high school, probably making all the cheerleaders swoon."

"Well, geez, when you put it like that…" he teased, tipping her chin up as he looked into her face, his smile softening. "You're more beautiful than any woman I've ever known. Hardly vintage, besides the difference in our ages is only a speck of time. My grandmother was seven years younger than my granddad."

"Somehow that seems different."

"Because she was younger? Don't tell me you're a closet sexist?" He gaped in exaggerated shock, and she laughed, wondering, and hoping, if maybe he wasn't right. Maybe she'd been holding too tightly on to the past, worrying about things that had become too important in her mind, but which really weren't all that big of a deal.

Maybe she did deserve a life, and love. She was still young enough to have the things she craved, a man in her life. A family? Her heart raced even considering the possibility of having children with Nathan. The idea of a future with Nathan poised temptingly on the horizon. Dare she?

She looked him squarely in the eye. She had to know, if she was going to even consider handing him her heart; her life.

"Nathan, what are we doing? What does all this mean?"

He took her glass, set it on the table and pulled her into his arms.

"Let me show you."

IN THE MIDDLE of the night, Nathan was lying by Jennie's side, restless and wide-awake. By all rights, he shouldn't be either. He'd finished another bottle of wine with Jennie in between bouts of passionate, fun and crazy lovemaking, pouring some of another very pricey vintage over her and licking it from every delicious slope of her skin.

She'd been completely open with him, and they'd connected on that deep level he'd always imagined existed, but had never experienced with any other woman. Without even trying, she'd reached into his soul.

She was sprawled on her stomach beside him, gloriously naked, and it was all he could do not to trace his hand up over the delicious curve of her backside, dip his hand down into the well of softness between her legs and begin all over again. It was tempting, he wanted her, yet he also needed the time to think, to sort out what he was feeling.

Who was this woman who was turning his life, and his heart, inside out? He was falling hard—hell, he'd been half in love with her before she accepted his invitation to dinner. Tonight, he'd just fallen the rest of the way. She was his completion, the only one who made him feel whole. His father had always talked that way about his mother, and told Nathan never to settle for anything less in the woman he married. To wait for the one that kept your blood moving.

But what did you do when you found her, and everything you shared was built on lies? Betrayal? What would Nathan do if she was guilty, if she really did have blood on her hands? It pained him to even consider it. Still, as much as it hurt, he also had to know.

Sliding quietly out of bed, he picked his jacket up from the desk chair and slipped the disc Norris had given him from the inside pocket. Grabbing his robe he went quietly into his office and closed the door, booting up his machine. He had to know.

JENNIE AWOKE to the smell of coffee and the warmth of sunlight streaming in over her face. At first, the sensations were disorienting, but it only took her a delicious moment or two to remember where she was. *Whom* she was with.

The memory of the night before brought her fully awake, and she smiled, stretching her well-worked muscles, her bare skin moving luxuriously against the softness of the sheets that smelled like him. Or, more accurately, like *them*. She laughed, actually laughed out loud into the room, feeling giddy. Stuffing her face inside a pillow, she inhaled deeply, soaking it all in.

Speaking of sensations, where was Nathan? She frowned, looking at the clock. He'd left a note by the small alarm clock, and she plucked it from the bedside table—he'd had to get in for an early meeting, it said. Since he hadn't wanted to wake her, he had left some takeout in the kitchen. She smiled. So he did have one classic bachelor trait after all— no food in the cupboards. She decided to take it as a definite plus that he didn't have romantic breakfast items at the ready.

Reality set in and she realized that she had to get to work, as well—and she hadn't thought to stop back at her place and get a change of clothes last night. Terrific—yet another mad dash. After Sarah had caught them in the hallway, there was no way she was setting herself up for another round of teasing by coming to work in the same clothes she'd met Nathan in the night before.

As much as she missed waking up with him today, she'd rather they showed up separately to work, anyway. He'd been right about trying to keep their intimacy as private as possible, at least in the short term. Even though Ian, EJ and Sarah had all met their soul mates on the job, their spouses were not also working at their side in the office. Ian's wife Sage owned her own security consulting firm, and Logan had left law enforcement long before he and Sarah were married. And of course, EJ was investigating Charlotte's role in an online lonely hearts scam when he met her. It changed things a little, and Jennie was unsure how Ian in particular was going to react. He put the performance of the team first, she knew, and she didn't want him thinking she or Nathan were too distracted to do their jobs effectively.

She shook her head, feeling a little dazed as she swung her feet over the edge of the rumpled bed, smiling again as she thought about seeing Nate at the office. Hell, she was in real danger of falling head over heels for him, and from the way he'd looked at her, touched her, made love to her, his feelings were strongly in play, too.

So far, neither of them had dared talk about anything deeper than physical attraction. And she wondered if he had been avoiding her question about where their relationship was going. Once they'd touched, conversation had gone out the window.

She'd felt something more. A sense of connection she couldn't recall feeling before, with any other man. And it was wonderful. It would be even better if he felt the same way about her. Her fears were receding as her hopes sprang forth, and she couldn't stop it.

After living in her personal prison for so long, she finally felt free, and why not? She wasn't a criminal; she had never done anything wrong, and yet she lived less freely than her murderous uncle. But that was all in the past, wasn't it, and she should be concentrating on the future.

After a quick shower, she threw on her clothes and grabbed the take-out bag, starting to munch on the half-warm breakfast sandwich while searching around the apartment for Nathan's computer. Since she was going to be late, she wanted to check her work e-mail before heading home for a quick change of clothes.

Humming happily as she sat down at the console and thought about what she had to do that day, the breath whooshed out of her in a sharp, sick gasp as she mistakenly clicked on the open window at the bottom of the screen, and a list of names and pictures—including hers—appeared. She clicked on them, but nothing happened—the files were not found. Raising a shaking hand to her brow, she forced herself to think. The files must have been left on the desktop but the source removed. A disc, perhaps.

Opening the drawer at the center of the desk, she saw a shiny CD thrown on top of sheaves of papers, and instinctively knew it was something bad. She popped it into the drive, holding her breath as the files loaded.

She just kept staring, and reading, her life literally passing before her eyes. Unsure how she was even able to move, she ejected the CD from the drive again and checked it for any identifying information— where had Nathan gotten this? *Where? From whom?*

There was nothing—it was a burned disc, copied information, with no identifying information, nothing that told her who'd given it to him. She read some more of the file left on the screen—a virtual telephone book of East Coast Mafioso, from minor contacts to major players. Histories, pictures, recent activity and locations.

There were only two possibilities for who would have this level of surveillance information: her own office, or the mob themselves. Nathan couldn't be working on any kind of legitimate case concerning the HotWires, or she would know about it. This was her area. So where had he gotten this disc? The possibilities made her blood run cold.

Some of the people listed were her relatives. Her brother Tony, even.

And she was there, too. It hit her with a second slam to the chest. Nathan knew who she was. He knew everything. He'd known everything all along.

The knowledge almost caused her to fall to the floor as she tried to stand, her knees buckling, as sickness churned in her stomach. She managed to run to the bathroom, her breakfast wrenched from her body, her heart breaking, her mind screaming at how she could be so *stupid.* So reckless.

There were so many clues that she'd just overlooked, and they all became clear now. His recent arrival with the team, his hometown being the same as hers, his pursuit of her, his subtle questions about her family and growing up—he had to be working for her uncle somehow.

Then why hadn't he just turned her over to her uncle and let them kill her months ago? Why all the games? There had to be some larger agenda, some reason why she wasn't just dead. She couldn't make sense of it, but there must be a reason. Bruno must have a plan. She'd figure it out later.

Unless it was just as simple as getting her into bed for the fun of it, for the conquest—maybe he'd wanted to play with her before turning her over to her family.

Her heart screamed *no* back at her. It wasn't

possible. Not Nathan. Not *her* Nathan. It had to be some horrible, horrible mistake.

The pain was unbearable. She wasn't sure she could breathe, or move, let alone figure anything out. Let alone care. How could she have let herself hope?

Darkness threatened to invade, but then her survival instinct kicked in. She took several deep breaths, splashed water on her face. She had to get out. Get away, as far away as she could. She'd prepared for this—she'd always known it could happen. She had another name, IDs, money. She could go at any time, though in some small part of her mind, she'd hoped she'd never have to.

As she gathered up her things, she called the office and left a message saying that she was sick in order to buy herself some extra time. She left the disc in the drawer just as she'd found it and put the screen back to rights. Then, on second thought, she clicked off the files, erasing them from the screen—he wouldn't remember leaving them open. That had been a mistake, and she couldn't risk him discovering she knew. He'd know she called in sick, and it wouldn't be hard to put two and two together, so better to try to fool him into thinking he was in the clear, and she hadn't seen anything.

Her hands were still shaking. If he knew she'd found it, it would just set him on her trail all the sooner. She couldn't contact the Federal Marshals—for all she knew, that's how he'd found her in the first place. It was obvious her uncle's tentacles had spread far inside federal circles. She'd take care of herself this time.

She had to vanish. This very second.

5

TONY CASTONE LIFTED himself off his lover's hot, nubile body and rolled over to the other side of the bed. The sex had been good; Gina was always good. Still he was distracted. He had a lot on his mind these days.

"Gina?"

"Yeah, baby?"

"What would you do if it were all over tomorrow?"

"You mean, like the end of the world?" she teased. He was having a hard time sharing her humor—he *was* talking about the end of the world in a way. The end of *their* world, or the way of life they'd known.

"No, I mean, the end of the family. If we all had to go and live regular lives, like regular people."

"You're crazy. That's not gonna happen."

"Look, Lou Maloso, Vince Valente, my dad, a lot of the big guys are dropping like flies. What if that happened to us? What would you do?"

She lifted up on one elbow, reaching over him for the pack of cigarettes on the table by his bed—hers, not his—he hated the things. She didn't answer right away, instead she blew out a long stream of smoke as she looked down at him with slumberous dark eyes, the cloud of brown hair that was usually so well styled a mess from their interlude.

He enjoyed bedding Gina—he'd known her since they were kids and though he couldn't claim to love her, it was more or less expected that they'd get together. Tony hadn't put a ring on her finger yet. It was expected he would eventually, which was why her father, Uncle Bruno's captain, didn't cut his balls off. She sighed out another stream of smoke, answering with a shrug.

"I don't know. I never think about that. I suppose I would just get married and have kids, pretty much what I want to do now."

"You don't want more than that?"

Tony, himself, had always thought he'd like to give his creative streak expression somehow. His grandfather had been a stone mason—an artist with tile and brick—before he'd gotten caught up in the business. Tony wondered what it would be like to be an artist. Maybe teach...

"Like what?"

"A career, college maybe?"

She made a face. Apparently her imagination was limited to what she did in the bedroom.

"Why? Listen, even if all those old guys got pinched or died, you'd just move up—you'd be the head."

She smiled slyly, stubbing out the cig and sprawling over him, her expression provocative. Tony wasn't under any illusions of her loving him, either. What she did love was the power he had, or the position he would have held someday when the old guys died off—if he weren't planning on bringing it all down around their ears.

He couldn't let Gina know that, though—he couldn't afford to create any suspicion, and had probably already said more than he should to her. On some level he wanted Gina to know what was happening, to warn her—just because he didn't love her didn't mean he didn't care at all. In the end Tony couldn't trust her. He couldn't trust anyone.

She crawled up on top of him, sliding her silky heat over his dick until her warmth and wetness made him hard. He was still a guy, and she was a knockout and had been his lover for ages. Yet in his heart he knew it was all wrong between them. Reaching up, he planted his hands firmly on her shoulders and gently pushed her off, shaking his head in refusal. She swore, throwing him a dirty look and bouncing off the bed in a sulk.

"Fine. Whatever. I gotta meet my sister for lunch anyway."

Gina was spoiled; she didn't like being told no. Well, she was going to have to get used to it, because if Tony had his way, life was going to change for all of them soon enough. He was making a big play— settling the score for what Bruno had done to his family. Gina's father would probably be nabbed with his uncle and the rest of them. Tony had been working on a plan, building relationships outside the local guys, and it was time to fish or cut bait.

He'd found Maria through his own secret efforts, and at that point his plan had formed—a way to end this madness that had nearly destroyed his family. It was risky, but what did he have to lose? Part of his plan was planting misinformation about Maria to try to "flush her out" by using the very people who'd been protecting her—it was a clever idea if a dangerous one. If everything worked according to plan Bruno would be taken out and his sister could finally come home, all in one fell swoop. Once he'd set this machine in motion it wasn't just him anymore—and he couldn't predict how the other players could mess things up. He had to believe it would work. It had to work.

He knew his apparent willingness to rat out his sister was how his uncle assessed his loyalty, and it was the only reason Bruno kept him around.

Tony knew he was playing with some serious fire—he knew where his sister was, what she did. Hell, he'd even seen her, watched her. He'd taken a "business trip" to Virginia just last month to see if it was really her, to see with his own eyes if he'd at long last found her.

When he'd seen her leaving work one afternoon at the Norfolk Police Department, he'd had to hold himself back. He'd wanted to run to her, to shake her for leaving them, for choosing to testify and putting her life in such danger she had to leave. And to hug her and never let her go again. To bring her home to their mother—after the trial, he'd promised her he would bring back her only daughter.

Making it look like he was setting Maria up when he was actually setting Bruno up was tricky. His uncle was far too well connected here for Tony to be able to move on him. He needed help from higher powers, and he needed to lure his uncle to a place where he'd be less protected. It was dangerous using Maria as the bait. She'd understand, he hoped.

As beautiful as Maria was, she was alone. He'd followed her for a day or so and saw there was no man, no children in her life. He could tell she was haunted. It showed in all of her movements. Graceful, but restrained, wary.

Holding the image of Maria in his mind, he closed his eyes as Gina left, slamming the door behind her good and hard. Her tantrums had stopped bothering him long ago. She was what she was, and just maybe she would find it in her heart to understand why he was doing this after it was over.

Relieved she was gone, and knowing if all went as he planned that this would be the last time he'd ever see her, he reached for the untraceable, prepaid cell phone he'd bought at the discount store and dialed his contact. One meeting should tell him what he needed to know. As the person he was calling picked up on the other end of the line, he realized that there was no turning back. He prayed that Maria, of all people, didn't get caught in the cross fire.

"YOU LOOK A LITTLE BEAT, Nate. Tough night?" Ian inquired casually from across the conference table, winking to EJ conspiratorially. Nathan saw it, and decided to ignore it. He was in too good a mood.

As it was, he was having a hard time concentrating on the work at hand—tracking down a group who'd been manufacturing false UPC codes and ripping stores off left and right. The real kicker was that they were somehow managing to disguise the thefts inside of the retailers' inventories. The clever thieves were a group of phreakers—hackers who specialized in cracking and manipulating phone systems. Not only were they able to change the UPC sticker on the products, they also managed somehow to get into the inventory systems and alter the codes there, as well. The sales discrepancies weren't found until figures were compared with weekly and monthly sales and inventory reports from the main offices.

It wasn't anything that hadn't been done before on a smaller scale—high school and college kids could get the technology to change UPC codes, and did so with annoying frequency. The amateurs often got caught after one or two tries at repricing popular items like iPods and video games, which was stupid in and of itself as these were items where price differences were easily caught.

Unfortunately, retail staff were often young, inexperienced, overworked or apathetic and careless, so many of the crimes were successful.

Nathan had barely had time to review all of the case files before he was itching to see Jennie. He fought the urge to swipe his hand over his face, knowing her scent still lingered on his skin—God, he was in so deep with this woman.

She had to be innocent, she just had to be. He glanced over at the door, wondering where she was. Laughter around the table yanked him out of his thoughts.

"What?" he inquired, seeing his colleagues' amused, knowing expressions.

"She called in sick." EJ tossed off the comment casually.

"Jennie's sick?" Nathan was immediately concerned. Jennie had been fine when he'd left her, asleep. She hadn't mentioned feeling ill last night.

"Gotcha." EJ grinned.

"Huh?" Nathan stared at him in consternation, then closed his eyes, realizing EJ hadn't said *who* had called in sick. His bosses obviously knew that there was something going on, and that Nathan hadn't spent the night alone. He closed his eyes, nodding. "Oh. Yeah, good one, EJ."

Judging from the looks on their faces, they didn't

have a problem with it, and were just looking to yank him around a little. Why had Jennie called in sick? Maybe she was just tired? But that didn't seem like her.

"How long has this been going on?" Ian inquired casually while passing out some new files.

"About a week."

"Hell, man, you've been salivating over her for months. Good for you." EJ nodded in his direction, but then his friendly green eyes narrowed a bit. "And you had better be good to her."

Nathan met EJ's gaze with a level one of his own. He knew there was a lot of history here, relationships that had formed long before he was on the scene. Maria—Jennie—was even godmother to EJ's daughter. He was the new kid on the block. It was natural for her friends to be protective. Still, it rankled him a little, especially since he knew that in the distant past, Jennie and EJ had been a little more than friendly. But that was long before EJ's wife, Charlotte had appeared, and before Jennie had joined the team.

Ian cleared his throat as he watched Sarah bust through the door, just short of late herself.

"Looks like all the HotWires' women are running late this morning."

"I'm not late." Sarah looked at her watch. "I have thirty seconds until the meeting starts. I would say that makes me exactly on time." She wrinkled her nose at Ian, sitting in the chair next to Nathan. "Jennie's late?"

"She's not coming in today. Seems she had a tough night…." EJ coughed as Nathan glared in his direction, and Sarah grinned.

"Yeah, I caught them in a hot clinch in the hall last night."

Nathan threw his hands up. "What? Is everyone monitoring my love life? Don't we have better things to do?"

Ian leveled them all a look that indicated fun time was over. "Yes, as a matter of fact, we do. Let's pull it together, people, and see what progress we've made on this case, and I want to hear what else you're working on."

Nathan maintained his composure—he was sure Ian would want to know what else he was working on, and though Nathan hadn't been part of the team for very long, he felt loyal to them. Lying to them, and lying to Jennie was starting to take its toll. He had to find a way to end this, and fast. He'd have to take a more aggressive approach, find out for sure that Jennie wasn't double-crossing them—because he knew in his heart that she wasn't. He'd better speed up his efforts to find proof. Then he could face her with a clear conscience.

"Uh, Nate?"

Nathan blinked, his attention snapped back to the issues at hand by Ian's annoyed tone.

"Sorry. What?"

"Why don't you go make a phone call and settle

your mind so you can concentrate. Then you can come back and contribute."

"I'm fine." Great. Now his boss was seeing him as a lovesick teenager who couldn't concentrate on his work without making a phone call to his girl-friend—the worst part was it was true. He had to remain professional. He'd call Jennie as soon as they were done here. It just motivated him to move through his presentation faster.

Nathan jumped in, all business. "There's defi-nitely a larger network in place—a group who accesses the internal systems, someone who deals with the physical reapplication of a UPC label, someone who did the buying and most likely someone who acts as their fence, to resell it. There have to be a number of them, and they change off, so you don't see the same person frequenting the stores over and over again."

"Video cameras catch anything?"

"Would if they'd had the cameras working."

"Dammit."

"Yeah. But it seems best to nail the hacking side of the operation first. There are probably only a few people, and maybe only one person, who would be working that side of it, so I've called in an expert, one of my old professors, Nolan Wagner, to see if he can consult. He's an expert in computer forensics, and he knows phone systems inside and out. If anyone can trace the intrusion, it's him."

"That name sounds familiar…." EJ's brow scrunched up as he tried to remember, and Nathan smiled as he thought about his former professor.

"You've probably seen him on TV or heard of him in the news somewhere. He was a kid genius—he was all over the media for a while, you know, Ph.D. at sixteen and all that. Every now and then they trot him out for a dog-and-pony show on daytime TV, or when the universities are trying to raise interest."

Nathan shook his head. "He's my age, for crying out loud, and he was teaching for five years before I sat in on one of his classes. I've never met anyone so brilliant. He's also a little, I don't know how to explain it, naive, I guess. About the world."

"Where's he teaching?"

"He's not. He had some clashes with the academic world a few years ago. I don't know much of what he's been up to since then—we've just kept in very minimal contact over e-mail. He seemed happy enough to come and help out. He should arrive tonight. I've set him up at a local hotel—the expense report is on your desk." Nathan grinned at Ian.

Nathan didn't include that his old friend and professor had been fired for teaching students how to hack into the college phone lines and make free calls home at the holidays. While Sarah or EJ might appreciate that humorous event, he didn't know what Ian, who was so much more straitlaced, would think.

In the usual way of creative, and largely harmless

hacker humor, the calls had been charged to the Dean's home phone number. They'd been easily rerouted back to the callers' accounts. Nolan had stood behind his students. In fact, he had applauded their creativity in public rather than apologizing. Being untenured, that had terminated his academic career.

Nathan wondered if Nolan hadn't been trying to find a way out of the ivory tower he'd been more or less locked up in since he was a child. He was looking forward to seeing Nolan. Nathan had liked him immediately, as a teacher and as a person. He also felt sorry for him; Nolan didn't seem to enjoy much interaction with the world outside of academia, and Nathan had always wondered if he'd ever even dated.

Ian nodded, satisfied. "Sounds good. Bring him in tomorrow, he sounds like an interesting guy. Let me know what progress we're making. What else?"

Sarah brought everyone up to date on her cases, and EJ was wrapping up the phishing case they'd been working on for months.

"Sounds like everything's on course. I'll talk to Jennie when she comes in, and if she has anything that bears on any of your cases, I'll catch up with you."

Everyone nodded, and the tone changed again as Nathan slid his cell phone out of his pocket, standing up without another word and heading out of the conference to take the call in private.

EJ laughed, looking after him. "It's about time those two got together."

Sarah chimed in. "Tell me about it. The lovesick look he's been wearing around for months is enough to make me puke. Ugh."

Ian shook his head, "How did I miss all this? This has been going on for months?"

"Right under your eyeballs, chief," EJ teased. "To their credit, they have been discreet, and haven't brought it into the workplace. Today was the first time I've ever seen Nate off his game."

"True," Sarah agreed.

Ian nodded thoughtfully, absorbing the comments. Love and work often seemed to go together among the HotWires team, even if it did make their work all the more complicated. And while Ian was always alert to anything that could throw the performance of his team off, he also had once fallen in love on the job, and it was the best thing that had ever happened to him. He couldn't be too critical about Nathan and Jennie, as long as their relationship didn't interfere with their work.

However, Jennie never got permanently involved with anyone, and for good reason, Ian knew. This affair could blow up in Nathan's face—it was clear that he was smitten—and Ian hoped they could maintain a professional relationship after the inevitable breakup happened.

"Stop worrying, Ian. It'll be fine," Sarah advised, knowing that once before her boss had worried about her ability to perform while on the job with a man she loved.

Ian nodded, standing and gathering up his files with a quick glance toward the door, where Nathan stood, making his call.

"I hope you're right."

JENNIE WASN'T FINE. She looked over her shoulder, sitting quietly in the bus station chair by the lockers, waiting and watching to make sure that no one was tracking her. She needed to get into one of the lockers and retrieve her escape cache—items she'd collected for this very kind of situation.

She felt numb right down to her soul; though she'd only been awake for a few hours, she was exhausted. Thankfully adrenaline and survival instincts had kicked in, giving her a much-needed boost of energy to keep going. She wasn't thinking about anything but how to get out. After calling in sick she'd grabbed some auburn hair dye and had changed her hair color in the YMCA bathroom—no one would think twice about her visiting there so early in the morning, since that's where she always went to work out.

She'd bought some nonprescription green contacts to alter her eye color and donned nondescript black pants, a black sweater and sneakers that she'd bought at the local discount store. At least from a distance, no one would recognize her.

Still she needed somewhere to go—somewhere untraceable, somewhere that she didn't need to register, use a credit card or even cash. She didn't know anyone she could contact; she'd have to wing it when she arrived.

She couldn't touch any of her bank accounts; they'd be tagged. A large withdrawal would signal that she was running. Once she got into the locker, she'd have what she needed to get out of town, and she would go from there. Everything she owned, even the few special things she loved, had been left behind; she didn't dare return to her apartment. Tears stung behind her eyelids and she blinked them away. She jumped when a low male voice addressed her, a hand landing on her shoulder.

"Hey! What are you…"

Jennie whirled around, setting the stranger back a few paces, his hands up in apology.

"Sorry, I thought you were someone I knew…."

Waiting for her pulse to stop slamming, she watched the man walk away and decided it was safe enough to approach the locker. She tried to look casual as she did so. How did her partners keep their cool so often working undercover? She didn't have much field experience, and she was trying to recall the basics as she went.

Amid all of the thoughts crowding into her mind, she pushed one back and refused to focus on it: Nathan. She couldn't think about him now, not yet, or she'd lose it.

She had to proceed carefully; at some point she'd need to contact EJ and let him know, warn him. But not until she was safe herself. She never would have figured Nathan for a dirty cop. Her friends were most likely safe until she could get word to them.

Her throat tightened painfully as she realized she would never see her second "family" again. Her little goddaughter would never remember her, and Charlotte and Sage would never be able to know the truth about who she was, or why she took off.

She never should have let herself get so involved with people. She'd known that. Now they'd all pay the price.

Reaching into the locker, she retrieved a paper envelope, exhaling in relief as no one seemed interested in her actions as she riffled through the contents, finding the fake IDs in the name of "Camille Jackson" and the wad of cash she'd stored away intact.

The package had been here for so long she'd almost forgotten about it—until she'd needed it. It was the one smart thing she'd done, preparing for contingencies that she'd prayed would never happen.

Looking up at the schedule, the next departure was to Pennsylvania. She frowned, wanting to head south; the next trip south didn't arrive for an hour, and left well after that. So, Pennsylvania it was. Buying a ticket, she found the bus just in time and took a seat close to the back, shutting her eyes and her heart to the life she'd come to love—to the people she'd come to love—as the bus doors closed with a hissing finality and pulled away from the curb.

NATHAN DIDN'T KNOW what was going on, but he knew it wasn't good. Jennie hadn't answered the phone at all—her cell or his home phone—and she wasn't returning his messages. He couldn't leave work; there was too much going on and he'd tripped over himself in front of the boss enough for one day. Still he couldn't shake the very bad feeling he had that something wasn't right with Jennie.

Maybe she was sleeping; maybe she had gotten sick and simply hadn't heard the phone or hadn't gotten up yet. Maybe she was at the doctor and had forgotten her cell phone. There were dozens of rational explanations, yet he couldn't convince himself to accept any of them.

When he finally wrapped things up and decided to hit the road early and find out what was going on, Detective Norris stopped him in the hallway, just short of the door.

The man's look was dark, his thick eyebrows crunched over his cold eyes, and he was more brooding than usual. The way he beckoned Nathan silently as he disappeared back into his office was ominous. Something was wrong, very wrong. Fighting the urge to run out the door and home, wanting to find Jennie and make sure she was okay, he turned and followed Norris inside the office.

Closing the door behind him, he faced Norris, and had to admit, the man looked haggard.

"She ran." Norris looked up at him accusingly.

"What I want to know is why—she must have made you, made us, but how? What aren't you telling me, Reilly?"

Nathan's mind was racing. He ignored Norris's question, homing in on one bit of information.

"What? Who ran?"

"Your *friend*. Who, by the way, appears to be much more than that according to the surveillance we had placed on you."

Although he was as far as a man could get from calm, he forced himself to sound matter-of-fact. "You were following me?"

Norris was unapologetic. "You bet. And it's a good thing we did. Lucky for you, aside from sleeping with your target, you look clean. She made you, Nathan, and now she's gone."

"Jennie's gone? Where?"

"We don't know. Our man lost her when he got caught behind a traffic accident downtown. She might have been heading to the bus station, we can't be sure."

Nathan stepped back, sitting down in the only other chair provided in the stark office. Evidently Norris didn't believe in creating a homey atmosphere at work.

"You've made a mistake. There has to be some explanation."

"There is. She found out she was about to be busted and took off. Question is, how'd she find out? Pillow talk?"

Nathan glared at Norris. He didn't have time to

mess with the jerk now; he had to know why Jennie had taken off. It just didn't add up; how could she have discovered his part in the investigation, and if she had, why would she flee?

Unless she *was* guilty, his mind echoed back at him.

"She didn't hear anything from me. I don't know what's going on, but I'm going to find out."

Nathan stood, barely noticing Norris's objections, and left. Driving much faster than he should have, he made it home in record time, and busted through the door of his apartment, not knowing what he expected to find, but finding…nothing. She wasn't there. Nothing was unusual or out of place. Closing his eyes in quiet realization he ran to his office, yanking open the drawer, and finding the disc IA had given him there, tucked away in the same place he'd left it. Nothing seemed out of place, yet the woman he was falling in love with had gone missing. He had to find out why.

When the phone rang, he grabbed it anxiously.

"Jennie?"

"Uh, no. Not quite. Nathan, it's Nolan. I'm at the airport, wondering where you are, bud."

Nathan passed a hand over his face; he'd completely forgotten about picking up Nolan. *Shit.*

"Listen, man, I'm sorry. I have something going on here; can you grab a cab? We can expense it for you."

"No problem—Nate, what's going on? You sound anxious."

That was the understatement of the year.

"I just had something blow up on me. I'm sorry we can't get together tonight. I told Ian and EJ about you, and they can meet with you tomorrow. Looking forward to it, in fact."

He eyed the doorway, barely listening to Nolan's response. With every second that ticked by, Jennie was getting farther and farther away.

"You sound stressed, Nate. I can meet you. Maybe I can help."

Nathan started to say no, then changed his mind. He could use all the help he could get.

"I'll come get you. You're right. I need some help on the q.t., Nolan. I can't talk about it on the phone, though."

"I'll be waiting, Nate."

He hung up, rushing out the door. He hated cutting Ian and EJ out of the equation, knowing there'd be hell to pay for it later. Worse, if he was wrong about Jennie. He had to do this his way, for the moment—and Nolan was maybe the only person he could trust, who he could tell. The only one who could help him find Jennie.

6

IT WAS CONSIDERABLY colder even just a few hours
north. The day was gray and wet, accentuating the
chill running down her spine. The leaves here had
already become an indiscriminate, brown mush on
the pavement, slippery under the soles of Jennie's
boots. Getting a coat and gloves was a priority, so
was food and a place to stay—she was starving,
weary and desperate to regroup.

As she looked around the bustling, busy streets of
Lancaster, she felt safe, if just for a moment. No one
would think to look for her here in the middle of
Amish country; the logical thing for her to do would
have been to head west or south. She would be okay
here long enough to formulate more of a plan.

Stepping into a diner, she rubbed her palms
together, warming her frigid skin. Delicious aromas
emanated throughout the small, simple space. She
found a blue vinyl-covered booth and sat, not
allowing herself to think past what she needed right
now. First food, then a place to stay. Some clothes
were next on her list, and most of all, a solid plan.

She couldn't afford the luxury of thinking about anything—or anyone—else, not yet. The time would come, her aching heart reminded her.

"Can I get you something, dear?"

"Coffee. A turkey sandwich, please."

"Shoofly pie is delicious today."

"Thanks, just the sandwich for now." Jennie cast a glance at the counter while the waitress wrote down her order. "Is that paper for anyone to look at?"

"Sure, here ya go, sweetie." The friendly woman grabbed the newspaper and slid it onto the table in front of Jennie.

She went immediately to the classifieds. She could do a motel tonight; what she really wanted was somewhere more private, where she could hide. The first place they'd look would be motels, and clerks were easily bought off.

The pickings were slim, and there was nothing she could get without going through an entire rental agreement process. She pushed the paper away, discouraged, as her sandwich arrived.

"You looking for an apartment?" the waitress inquired, looking at the exposed classified ads.

"Just a room would be fine. I won't be here for long. I don't want to stay in a motel."

The waitress nodded emphatically. "Not safe for a young woman traveling alone. Are you a student?"

"No, just passing through."

"On your way to…?"

Nosy, Jennie thought. Still, if she were too offish, she'd stand out. This wasn't the big city; people didn't see their questions as nosy so much as friendly. Part of the charm.

"Visiting family in Maine, but making a lot of stops along the way, seeing the countryside." The lie slipped easily from her lips. Now if anyone asked after her, they would get nothing but misinformation.

"Well, this is a tough time of year. A lot of B and Bs are closed down, and the students are back, taking up all the rooms. There is a nice inn down the street which costs a mint."

Jennie smiled, picking up her sandwich as a signal to the woman that the conversation was over.

"Thanks, I'm sure I'll figure something out."

Not more than two seconds later, she was back.

"Wait, I just remembered something. I heard that Marge Sawyer's boyfriend—who was really just a lazy waste of space—finally left for good. So she might have some room. She's a nice girl, teaches at the college, about your age. Would you like her number? You could tell her Angie told you about a room. She might even let you stay for free."

Now Jennie felt bad for lying, because this was just what she needed.

"Is it close by?"

Angie shook her head. "A little outside the city limits. It's a beautiful little farmhouse, Marge's mother left it to her. The buses run by there all the time. It's easy enough to get to."

Jennie held her breath. This could work out—a place just outside of town would be great—less likely anyone would spot her there, if anyone was looking. And she was sure they were by now. She'd covered her tracks, then again, she'd thought she was safe before, too. And if Nathan was looking for her, and if he was using HotWires' resources to find her…she couldn't be too careful.

"Do you have a phone I could use?"

"You just come along with me. It's close to night-time, and I don't want a pretty girl like you out there with nowhere to stay. It's a nice town, but you can still run into trouble."

Jennie took a deep breath. If Angie only knew.

NATHAN WAS HAPPY to see his former professor, and wished the pleasure wasn't dampened by his worry over Jennie. Where could she have gone? And why? His mind was spinning with all the questions, anxiety tensing every muscle in his body. Had it been only twenty-four hours ago—less—when he'd been holding her next to him, loving her?

"So, are you going to tell me what the deal is?"

Nathan looked over at his friend, who looked very different than he had back in school. Nolan was always a cool guy. Back then it had been in a repressed, academic kind of way. Clark Kent kind of cool.

He'd been brilliant, and that was his claim to fame, literally. Now, though, he just looked more like, well, a regular guy. Decked out in his faded leather jacket, slick wire-frame glasses and beat-up jeans, his blondish hair—hadn't it been brown back then?—slightly spiked, and longer than it was before, he didn't appear even remotely academic. What had initiated the change? That discussion would be for another time.

"I'm trying to find someone."

"Criminal?"

Nathan stopped at a red light, acknowledging the question with a curt nod. "Maybe."

"Are we working through your unit? What are they called again?"

"The nickname that stuck is the HotWires…you know, like the nickname for the elite firefighting teams out west, the Hot Shots? It's a computer crime task force, linked to local police departments. We share resources, even though we function separately."

Nathan pressed the gas pedal again, turning in the direction of the bus station, following up on the one vague lead that Norris had given him. "And, no, we're not working through the department. Not at the moment."

"Interesting. I knew there were federal bureaus all over. Addressing computer crime at the local level makes sense. So why aren't you working through the department? Personal grudge?"

"Something like that."

Filling the silence, Nathan explained his assignment with IA, his relationship with Jennie and what had happened. It felt good to get it off his chest, really. By the time he turned into the parking lot of the station, Nolan was sitting quietly, pondering what he'd been told.

"You have no idea why she ran?"

"Nope. All I have is the little bit of a lead that she'd been heading in this direction. Frankly, she's smart, and she's been at this for a long time. She wouldn't be that easy to track."

"So how can I help?"

Nathan got out of the car, slanting him a smile that didn't have a whole lot of humor in it. "Well, for one thing, you're unofficial, and I needed someone to bounce ideas off. There's no one like you, with that brain you're carrying around."

Nolan laughed, and they walked toward the station doors.

"And I know you have the technical expertise—I have some, but it could take more to find her."

"And you can't turn to your unit seeing as you were indirectly investigating them, as well, for IA?"

"Yeah, pretty much. Needless to say, they'll be pissed. EJ and Ian would probably yank me off of this case so fast I wouldn't know what hit me, and I have to find her. I have to know what's going on. I can't just sit back and watch others go after her."

"Could she have found out about you? That would explain why she didn't come to you first, which is the most logical thing for her to have done. She was at your place, and there's no evidence she went back to her apartment, right?"

Nathan nodded as Nolan continued in a speculative tone, "And yet she didn't come to you, didn't even call you—don't you think that's odd? If you were in trouble, wouldn't you go to the person you love and trust the most first?"

Nathan winced; he didn't know if Jennie loved him, though they'd definitely been moving in that direction. It was obvious she didn't trust him, and with good reason, really—though she wasn't supposed to know that, either. Was it possible she'd found the disc? But why leave it behind? Why not confront him?

"You're right, as usual. It makes sense that she might have found out. So why not confront me, tell Ian and EJ, have a fit, whatever? Okay I'm investigating her. That still doesn't account for why she would run."

"Unless she was guilty." Nolan stated the obvious answer to Nathan's question flatly.

"Yeah, it always seems to end up back there. Either way, I have to have answers."

They approached the security offices located at the back of the building. This wasn't where the lost and found was located or where lost children went, but where the video monitoring was done and stored. Usually only the police and inside staff knew about the internal security offices, and that they weren't usually manned by more than a few people.

"Do you have a contact here?"

"No. We can't go in under an official mandate, or they could tip EJ or Ian off. I have a plan, though."

"I figured you would. What do you need me to do?"

"Play along."

"Sounds like fun."

Nathan crumpled his collar a little, and ran a hand through his hair. He already looked haggard from worry, so that was a given. Nolan stood next to him, his own brow furrowed in what looked like intense concern. Nathan stepped forward, not knocking, instead walking directly into the office, his step forceful. The older man sitting at the desk on the other side of the door started, narrowing his eyes and standing, and began to speak. Nathan cut him off.

"I need your help. Please. Just listen for a moment."

"You're not supposed to be in here. If you have a problem or a complaint, you need to go—"

"Listen, I've asked everyone. No one will help. My sister has been missing since this morning. She's ill, she needs medicine. She—" he sighed, wiping his hand over his face "—she tends to take off. She doesn't know what she's doing. The cops won't do anything for twenty-four hours. They say she's an adult, and she's not really missing until then. I've been everywhere. I have to find her. I need to see if you can see her on a tape from this morning."

"I'm sorry, sir, you have to leave. I'll have to call an officer if you don't. Only the police can…"

Nathan kept his cool, subtly searching the office for something he could use—the guy was good at his job. At the last second, he saw a thick envelope on the counter, a few pictures strewn over the Formica shelf, one of which had a young woman in it. From her features, he guessed a granddaughter. Reaching over, he picked it up, smiling slightly.

"Yours?"

The man pulled back, obviously annoyed, but nodding stiffly. "That's our granddaughter Regina. Her seventeenth birthday party."

Nathan held the picture for another minute and stared at it, then Nolan quietly took it from his hand and handed it back to the guard, stating coolly, "How would you feel if she went missing and no one would do anything about it?"

Nathan saw that they'd breached the barrier. The guy was weakening.

"Here's her picture. My sister." He pulled out the framed photo he'd snatched from Jennie's table, a picture of her and EJ's children. "I know you can't show us the tapes. Could you look and see if you can spot her on the footage from this morning? If we just have some clue where she was going…maybe what time she was here. I need to find her."

The desperation in his voice was real; there was no need to act when it came to how much he did need to find Jennie.

"Okay, I can look. You take a seat."

Nolan and Nathan shared a covert glance of relief. They stood anxiously by the counter as the man returned behind the glass. It wasn't long until he emerged again, a still shot in his hand. Nathan's heart leaped.

"This looked like her. The hair is wrong—hard to tell in black and white, and it's grainy. The features seem right. I printed it out for you, so you have something more recent. That's all I can do. The time in the corner says she was seen at the counter around eleven o'clock."

Nathan looked down at the picture of Jennie standing at the ticket counter—the guy was right— her hair didn't register as dark as it should have, and she was dressed down, definitely trying to remain unnoticed. She held a ticket in her hand.

"Any way to find out who sold her this ticket?"

The guard shook his head. "That employee is gone for the day, and you'd need a police order to get more information. Sorry, son, this is all I can do for you. Good luck finding her."

Nathan shook the man's hand, thanked him for his help, then they left the office.

"So she was here, and she's long gone now. How the hell can we find out where?"

Nolan smiled, taking the photo from Nathan's hands.

"Piece of cake."

JENNIE STOOD AT THE END of the walk, cold through to her bones, staring at the charming building before her. Although it was dark, she could still appreciate the beauty of it. The farmhouse was situated a few miles outside the city limits, on the edges of what everyone referred to as "Amish country," where tourists got caught behind locals driving horse-pulled wagons on the roads. The traditions and ways of life in Amish communities were so very different from the rest of the country.

She wished she had more time to explore the area. Instead she hustled her way up to the porch, looking forward to the warmth the golden cast from the windows promised. She knocked, the cold wood of the door painful on her icy knuckles, and forced a smile when the door opened. She probably looked like hell. She didn't want to scare poor Marge Sawyer, who had sounded like a really nice person on the phone.

She looked as nice as she sounded, a small, rounded blond woman, so pale even the long lashes framing her pretty blue eyes were blond, creating a sort of ethereal look. Jennie held out a hand as she stepped forward.

"Hi, I'm Camille Jackson. Thanks so much for taking me in."

Marge smiled. "You're welcome. Angie is a sweetheart, isn't she? I'm glad she thought to send you here. I don't mind the company, actually."

Jennie didn't want to pry into the woman's business or her recent breakup, instead she eyed the stack of male clothing and sports gear stacked haphazardly in the corner of the entryway.

"I heard you had a room available, and I'm willing to pay what I can. It will only be for a few days. I really appreciate it."

Already the warmth was seeping into her bones and the scent from the woodstove was heavenly.

"You're welcome as long as you like, and whatever you can afford is fine," Marge said, closing the door. "I was thinking about taking in a student. Since the buses run by, it would be possible. This will give me a dry run to see how it works out. It's nice to have another woman around for a change."

Jennie eyed the stack of belongings again.

"Yes, I heard, uh, that…"

Marge laughed and appeared amazingly good-humored for a woman who'd just suffered a romantic breakup. In fact, Jennie almost burst out laughing when her new landlord glared at the stuff menacingly and then in a purely childish but somehow female gesture, stuck her tongue out at the pile.

"I take it the previous tenant didn't remember to take all of his stuff?"

"Oh, Camille, the stories I can share if you're interested. I don't know why I stuck with him for so long. The love, and the lust for that matter, faded long ago. I feel like I've lost about one hundred and seventy pounds!"

Marge laughed. Buoyed by Marge's good humor, Jennie found herself envying the woman's practical outlook. Losing Nathan felt more like losing a major organ, she thought, then clamped down on the wave of emotion that threatened.

"Well, I'm glad it wasn't a bad breakup."

"Bad for him—best move I ever made. All this stuff was clogging up the guest room—I hauled it out when I got your call. He's coming by to pick it up. I should leave it out on the front yard."

Sighing dramatically, Marge smiled again, taking Jennie by the arm. "Come along up here, I'll show you the room. I have some dinner, a good part of an Italian sandwich and some salad left over if you're hungry. Or you can just use the kitchen and get yourself whatever you want. Help yourself. The room is small, but it's clean. The house is at your disposal."

Jennie followed her up the stairs, just absorbing her chat. Marge really did like to chat. It was nice, still Jennie suddenly felt the overwhelming need to be alone, to just collapse.

"Here it is. You make yourself at home. Bathroom is down the hall. You look like a hot shower and a nap wouldn't hurt you any. Do you have a jacket?"

Jennie smiled, feeling foolish. "I was coming from the south, and I didn't think ahead for the weather."

"Wait here for a sec…."

Marge skipped down the stairs and reappeared a few seconds later holding a black parka; Jennie recognized the brand and knew it was an expensive jacket.

"Here, take this one."

"Oh, I can't take your jacket…."

Marge smiled slyly. "It's not mine—it was *his*. It may be a little big. You're tall, so it could fit well enough to keep you warm. I gave it to him for last Christmas, and he never wore it, said it was too fancy. Some mumbo jumbo about supporting the capitalist machinery or whatever. He was studying Marxism at the time, I guess. Well, let me tell you he'll be missing it when the cold weather hits, and I hope he freezes his useless little Marxist balls off."

Jennie blinked and could only stare, holding the jacket and watching her new benefactor move gaily back down the stairs, leaving a little trail of friendly chat and invitations to join her for tea behind her.

Jennie hoisted the heavy jacket up over her arm and closed the door behind her. She turned on a light by the dresser and relaxed at the sight of the comfortable room. The thick quilt on the bed was handmade, she could tell by the intricate stitching, and she wasn't surprised—this was quilting country after all. She made a note to ask Marge about the meaning of the design.

The furniture was heavy oak, thick and sturdy designs that made everything feel so solid. She was drawn to it, since nothing much felt solid in Jennie's world at the moment. Staving off any thoughts she set down her backpack, and let her sore muscles unwind. It felt as if she'd been on the road for a week, not merely one day.

Sliding up on the bed and closing her eyes for a moment, she sank back against the headboard, avoiding her reflection in the large oval antique mirror that stood by the dresser, while she thought about her next move.

She needed to talk to Ian and EJ, to let them know what she knew and why she'd run, though not before she could find a safe way of doing so. She knew her colleagues wouldn't sit by and take her news sitting down; they would try to find her. So she had to make sure she couldn't be found.

She'd trashed her cell phone in case they were using it to track her, which would probably be their first move. She'd gotten too comfortable, and sloppy. From now on she couldn't even risk the permanence of a regular cell phone—she'd have to rely on disposable, untraceable ones. At least until she settled in somewhere, maybe even outside of the States, and cultivated Camille's new life.

Another new name. This one a little closer to her heritage, but farther away from who she really was. She was smothering under the false identities that were necessary to save her life.

Opening her eyes and facing her pale reflection in the mirror, she wondered, what life? What about her life was so wonderful it was worth all this trouble?

No, she couldn't think like that. If nothing else, the religious training of her youth convinced her of two things: life was precious, for one, and we were never handed any trial we couldn't handle, for another. At the moment, however, she wasn't so certain of that.

The wave of emotion that had been building threatened to overtake her the more she brooded about her predicament, and she wouldn't be able to fight it for long. Nathan's image came to mind, his mossy-green eyes, his full sensual lips. She ran her hands up her arms, still too close to remembering his touch, and bit her lip hard. She'd been holding back all day, and everything was coming to a head now.

She couldn't risk having Marge hear her, so she dropped her bag and hustled down the hall to the shower. Closing the door, she stripped quickly, turning the hot water on full. Stepping in, she sank down on the tile floor, the drumming of the stinging spray absorbing the sobbing sounds of her shattered heart.

NATHAN PULLED UP in front of his apartment building, discouraged and wanting to hit something. Hard.

So, they knew Jennie'd left town on a bus—they still had no clue where to. Just because she was at the ticket counter around eleven o'clock didn't mean anything—she could have booked a trip for any time during the afternoon, though it stood to reason that she would want to leave as soon as possible. Even so, that left four or five possible routes according to the bus schedule.

Nolan had charmed one of the women at the counter into looking for her name on a sales record, despite the fact it was against the rules. Nolan seemed to have developed a way with the women, Nathan noticed. No one named Jennie Snow had passed through the gates—she'd been using a fake identity, no surprise there. There was no way to tell what it was unless they could get the passenger list, and go through each name. Which they couldn't do without a warrant.

Nathan slid a look in Nolan's direction.

"You asleep?"

Nolan's head was bent down, and he held the picture the security guard had given them. He was either staring at it, or sleeping.

"Hardly. Can you get into your offices at night?"

"Sure. Why?"

"I wonder if we could blow this up and see what we could see."

"Like what? The resolution is shit."

"I have some software that works miracles filling in gaps on bad or damaged pictures and video—smart photo software. I've been developing it with a friend. I need a machine powerful enough to run it on."

"You see something there we might home in on?"

"Maybe we could see what's printed on that corner of the ticket that's showing."

Nathan sat back, incredulous. "You're kidding me. You can see something like that?"

Nolan shrugged. "The software still has some bugs. It was developed for just this kind of thing. Worth a try."

"Absolutely." Nathan threw the car back in drive, and in a few short minutes they pulled into the office lot. Fortunately both Ian and EJ's parking spots were empty. He didn't need the hassle right now.

"Nice digs. You must be doing pretty well," Nolan commented as they walked off the elevator, looking around. Nathan just grunted, wanting to get to the lab to see what they could see, and get out again.

"Yeah, the unit's been a success. They're popping up new ones all over."

"Holy crap…" Nolan's voice was filled with awe as they walked into the lab, a space off the main offices filled wall to wall with every kind of computer technology available. The room literally hummed.

"Will this do?"

"I'm sure of it."

"You're glazing over, Nolan."

"You just have a lot of neat toys here, buddy."

"I know. Work now, play later."

"Fair enough."

Nathan led Nolan to a computer with a screen that rivaled many large-screen video setups, and pulled out a chair. Nolan didn't waste any time loading up his software from his home-office computer and getting to work, scanning in the photo. It wasn't long before he waved Nathan over from where he'd been pacing.

"Okay, see that?"

Nathan studied the large image—some parts had been completely pixelated, and couldn't be recognized as anything at all, not even shapes. A few spots, however, were strikingly clear.

"We can isolate parts of the photo or video, and manipulate the pixels. The software reads the logic of the image, essentially, to find out what's missing, and tries to replace it—and we can manipulate it as we go until we see something that more or less makes sense."

"Amazing." He leaned in, studying the corner of the ticket receipt Jennie held. All he could see was a part of a number. Three. And maybe the start of a two.

Whipping out his copy of the bus schedule, he scanned for what route numbers had been departing the station between eleven and one, and which had those numbers identifying them. Knowing routes changed and were canceled all the time, he called the bus station for confirmation, and after a few minutes, hung up with a feeling of victory.

"Only one bus actually left between eleven and one—there was a weather problem that held things up, and all the schedules were off, but one bus left."

"For where?"

"Lancaster, PA. Bus 328."

"Sounds like a good bet, though it still could end up being a wild goose chase."

"Could be."

All the same, his gut was telling him it would take him exactly where he needed to be.

7

JENNIE SAT ON THE SOFA with a cup of tea she'd brewed in Marge's cozy kitchen. Marge was upstairs getting ready for work. Her host knew something was wrong, and had looked at her with marked concern, solicitously making her breakfast. She'd been sensitive enough not to press.

Jennie was thankful for that. She'd slept hard for a good part of the night, exhausted and discouraged. Upon waking, she knew she couldn't stay here for long.

It was the kind of place she'd love to have for herself, and she envied Marge a little. The house was peaceful and quaint, and was filled with keepsakes. Over breakfast, Marge had pointed out the wall hanging sewn by her grandmother that she was particularly fond of, and the yellowware bowl collection that her mother always said should be used and not just looked at. There was something handmade in every corner, and on every wall, it seemed.

This was the part of the country where some families did everything by hand; where the Amish lived good, solid lives completely without modern "conveniences," Jennie mused.

If she had more time, she would be interested in learning more about that; she'd sat in front of a computer for most of the day for almost half of her life. What else would she have done with those hours, those days? It had been her work, sure. Had there been more that she'd missed? Had she been escaping from the lonely life she led by anesthetizing herself in front of a computer screen?

Her life was in flux at the moment, though the upside was that now she could go wherever she wanted, do something new. Be someone new. Still, the idea didn't carry much attraction.

"Hey there. You ready?"

She was hitching a ride to campus with Marge, so that she could use a campus computer and library resources to plot her next move. She also had to e-mail EJ and Ian to warn them about Nathan.

Since you could only use a campus computer with a student or faculty account, Marge had offered the use of hers. Jennie had refused. She felt bad enough lying to Marge, as it was. Besides a faculty e-mail account would have the name of the school in the address—EJ and Ian would locate her in five seconds.

She needed to find a student who had a generic Web account, hard to trace to the college without considerable effort. It should be easy enough to find some e-mail account left open in a computer lab since busy, tired students often didn't have enough presence of mind to close before they left.

"All set?"

Marge came down the stairs, looking fresh and professional in a brown wool suit, and Jennie wished they could get to know each other better. As much as she liked Marge, with any luck she'd be gone in a day or two, and it was better not to forge any connections. For Marge's safety, too.

"I am. This tea is wonderful; thanks so much for everything, including the ride into town."

She grabbed the heavy jacket Marge had lent her—it was a great coat—and joined her on the walk to the car.

"Is all this farmland yours?"

"Oh, no. Only over to that stand of trees, there." She pointed to a line of trees about a half mile from the house. "The rest is all working farm, not mine. The neighbors don't mind if I use it—I go for walks all the time out there, you can lose yourself in thought while you walk and not have to worry much about where you are. It's nice."

Jennie nodded in silent agreement, belting herself into the passenger seat. She didn't really have much to say beyond small talk, so she just stared out the window at the prewinter landscape, the farms tucking in for the cold weather.

"So have you ever been to Maine?" Marge asked, clearly liking to talk as she drove.

Jennie shook her head. "No, this will be my first time."

"You might want to shop for some warmer clothes. It will be twice as cold up there, you know. There's a great secondhand store near campus...." She stopped, holding her gloved hand to her pink lips. "Oh, I mean, not to say that you have to shop for seconds, I mean, I'm sure you have—"

Jennie laughed a little and smiled reassuringly. "I'm fine. I may do a little shopping, and I love thrift shops. I rummage through them all the time. If you can point it out, I'll definitely stop by. I just wanted to travel light, and until I got this far north it wasn't a problem."

She was also glad to know there was a place she could shop close by. She needed to lie low, still. Even if no one was likely to be looking for her here, it wasn't good to be seen all over town. A second-hand shop would be perfect, and she could blend in around campus.

"I just speak before I think sometimes. This place really is great—all the students trade in their stuff there, so you can get some great fashions. I think my students have more money than I do. Most of them drive nicer cars," Marge said, as they merged with heavier traffic.

They laughed, and Jennie decided it couldn't hurt to engage in conversation. And she wanted to be friendly; it was the least she could do considering how nice Marge was being to her.

"So, I guess since I'm wearing this jacket and the

previous owner is somewhere freezing his balls off, that this breakup is for good?"

Surprisingly, Marge laughed. "You mean Angie didn't give you all the details?"

"No, she did mention you had 'finally unloaded the loser,' though."

Marge sighed. "Yeah, and this time it is for good. I swear. His name was Chris, and he's a Ph.D. student at the college—has been for about nine years now."

Jennie looked over at her. "Nine years? I didn't think it took that long to get a doctorate."

"It doesn't. He's just one of those guys, you know? Handsome, smart, and knows how to play the enlightened male card—he has that academic gloss that can be reassuring until you look a little deeper. He's really just a user. He uses the school as a place to feel like he's doing something with his life when he's not, and he used me to… Well…he used me for a lot of things."

Her voice was completely devoid of self-pity or drama, Jennie noted, just stating what was.

"It sounds like you're much better off without him."

"That's a grand understatement. Except I hate that I took him back after breaking up with him so many times. I hate that I was so susceptible. It wasn't so much being gullible, it was just that I needed some of what he offered—the compliments, the companionship…."

She laughed lightly, then sighed again. Jennie nodded, trying to offer some comfort.

"We all have needs that make us susceptible. Too

bad there are so many men willing to take advantage of that."

The last words came out on a slightly more bitter note than she intended, and Marge cast a knowing glance in her direction.

"I guess it's something we've all been through."

The statement really was a gentle inquiry, Jennie knew. What could she share? That she was on the run from her Mafioso uncle who wanted to kill her? That the man she'd made love with only a little more than twenty-four hours ago was a dirty cop working for organized crime, and was probably hunting for her right now? That Marge's life could be in danger just by being around Jennie?

Not likely. She stared back out the window, murmuring, "Yeah. We all make some pretty stupid mistakes."

She felt Marge's hand on her elbow, and turned to meet her sympathetic gaze as they paused at an intersection. Marge was an extroverted, friendly woman. She was also smart.

"Jennie, if there's something you need to talk about, you can trust me. Even if it's something bad. Is there someone bothering you? Was he abusive? You look like you've been through the wringer, if you don't mind me saying so, and I…"

Jennie wondered at her hesitation, and became wary. "What?"

"I heard you last night—you sounded like you were crying."

Damn. The shower had obviously not been loud enough to cover up her sobbing. Jennie just smiled; she wasn't about to drag this very nice woman into her troubles.

"Thank you, I'm fine really. All ancient history, every now and then, it just gets to me. That's why I left and I'm going to find someplace new to stay. To start fresh." Well, at least that much was true.

"Well, if you ever want to talk, I'm here."

"Thanks. Same goes." She lightened the moment, getting off of that topic. "What do you teach?"

"I'm an Associate History Professor. Half of my courses are in Women's Studies, centering mostly on women's history, women's issues."

"Sounds wonderful. I wish I'd taken something like that when I was in college."

Marge smiled. "It's never too late."

Jennie returned an agreeable smile, even as she thought that sometimes it really was.

TONY EMERGED from the T-station near Government Center. He passed by a busy Starbucks as he made his way through the throng of people moving along the busy Boston street.

The conversations from the last hour were still buzzing through his head. Everything was set in motion now. He just had to do his part, which he planned to initiate ASAP, after he made one last stop.

He'd walked instead of driving—taking the

subway and walking made him harder to follow, just in case. It wouldn't draw suspicion. The nice thing about the city of Boston proper was that you could cover it end to end on foot if you wanted, and he often left his car in the garage when he was conducting local business.

Now, he headed with a sure step toward the North End, toward the family home he'd grown up in. The Castones had lived along the narrow streets and busy neighborhoods of Boston's oldest neighborhood, within blocks of the Old North Church and Bunker Hill, for the past eighty years, since his great-grandfather had come over from the old country and opened a cheese shop on Salem Street.

Papa had been part of the original "organization," and each generation of Castones had followed in his footsteps, positioning them as one of the major crime families in the area. Tony meant to see to it that it ended with his generation.

He had his own home across town, by one of his favorite places in the world: Fenway Park. A small apartment with a great view of the ballpark; he turned down his uncle's offer of a luxury apartment in one of the upscale waterfront condos Bruno had a hand in building. Tony wasn't home all that much anyway. His apartment was just a place to go, his real home was the quaint walk-up with the brightly painted red door and the potted plants on the stoop. He skipped quickly up the stone steps, and let himself in.

"Mama? You here?"

He smiled broadly when his mother—all of five foot one yet one of the most strong and intimidating women he'd ever met—came bustling around the corner, flour all over her apron and hands, her joy at his unannounced visit obvious. She kept her wavy dark hair stylishly short now, and her brown eyes danced, her smile widening when she looked over his face. She'd been an Italian beauty who'd stopped traffic when she'd crossed the street, his father used to say, and aging only deepened the character of her face, the wisdom in her eyes. He'd seen too much sadness there over the years, as well.

"Tony! What a nice surprise!"

Flour-covered hands grabbed his cheeks and pulled him down for a sound kiss, and he felt some of the stress from the day fade to the background. This was what he was risking everything for.

"I can only stay a little while. What are you cooking now?"

"Come in and have something while we talk. I just made *Timbale di Riso* and I have too much. And you missed lunch."

He stood back and looked at her in amazement. "How do you know these things?"

She swept a glance over him, placing her hands on her hips. "I can tell when my boys aren't eating."

Boys. His heart twisted a little bit. She still referred to them in the plural, even though Gino was years gone.

"I'll sit, only for a few minutes, though."

"That's all I ever hear from you these days. Just a few minutes. You know, you should slow down, make your minutes count—there are only so many of them each of us get here on this earth, Tonio."

"I know, Ma, I know. Hey, not so much." He laughed as she piled a plate deep with fragrant risotto rice and pastas filled with meats and cheeses, and then relented as she steadfastly ignored him. His stomach rumbled; it was the first time he'd been really hungry in days. Anxiety was stealing his appetite, eagerness to get things done and over with.

"I just put the bread in the oven, it won't be done for an hour," she chatted on, taking a smaller portion and joining him at the table. The eagle-sharp eyes pinned him, though, as he started to eat. "What's wrong?"

He looked up, feeling twelve and caught up to no good, and shrugged, feigning innocence.

"I'm just eating. This is amazing, mama. You are the best cook on the planet."

She smiled, soaking in the praise. Nevertheless, she was too sharp to be sidetracked by flattery.

"Tonio, ever since you were little, you made that face when you were worried—or in trouble."

"What face? I'm not making any face."

The glare she sent him was an order to cut the crap; nothing had changed. He didn't want to drag her into this mess. Still she deserved to know. And she was perhaps the only person in the world he could trust.

"I think I found Maria, Mama."

The fork his mother held clattered to the tile floor, and she didn't bother to retrieve it, so he did. She looked at him, pale, terror in her eyes.

"You mean, Bruno knows? They…"

"No, no." He grabbed her hand across the table and squeezed. "No, he doesn't know. Not yet. She's well, mama. Beautiful, like you."

His mother's eyes welled, and she immediately pulled the emotions back in, though her grip on his fingers was like a vice.

"You've seen her? With your own eyes?"

He smiled reassuringly. "Yes, with my own eyes. She's done well, all things considered. She has a good job, she has friends."

"A husband? Children?"

"No, you know she would never risk that. She could never have that kind of life knowing Bruno would never stop looking for her."

"How did you find her? If this is so, she is able to be found. What if…?"

"Bruno will find out. I have to tell him."

"No!" She wrenched her hand away, looking at him as if he were the devil himself, and drew her hand back, no doubt to slap some sense into him. He grasped her hand midair, and eased it back down.

"Mama, let me finish. This is the only way. I have a plan, to keep Maria safe, to bring her home."

"You can't keep her safe. Bruno will kill her on sight. Or worse."

"I know. I'll take care of Bruno."

Their eyes connected and she shook her head desperately.

"No, Antonio, no. No more killing. Even if you kill Bruno, his men will just kill you, and Maria, then there will be no one. No one left. At least I've had the comfort of having you and knowing she was out there somewhere, safe from *him*." She stood, her hands shaking as she went back to the steaming casserole on the stove. She looked at it, then him, smiling sadly.

"I always make too much, I know. Cooking for all of you for so many years, two strong boys and a husband with a good appetite. I can never seem to make just a little…."

"Mama, don't. Please." He rose, wrapping his arms around her petite frame. "It will work out. I'm going to end this once and for all, and you will have your daughter, my sister, back. She will have her life back. I'm going to end this for all of us. We can have a normal life, Mama. Not like before."

"Ah, Tonio." She shook her head, holding him, too, and he could feel her fear. Fear that she was going to lose the last of her children. "And how exactly are you going to make this miracle happen?"

He smiled disarmingly, looking into her face until she smiled a little, too, and kissed the top of her head. She didn't need to know details; the less she knew, the better. His voice was soft,

"I heard Victor Basile lost his job the other day. He's on disability from an injury. Why don't you bring some of this to his family? They'll appreciate the good meal."

She smiled, patting his arm.

"You're a good boy, Tony. That's a good idea."

"I'll be gone for a few days, Mama. You hear anything, don't listen. Anyone asks, you pretend you don't know anything. You wait to hear from me. Everything is going to be fine. I promise."

She reached for his plate, never dropping her gaze from his. "I'll wrap this for you, put it in the freezer until you get back."

He smiled. "I'll look forward to it."

With one last glance, Tony told his mother he loved her, and walked back out through the shiny red door into the street, heading toward the shop where Bruno waited in his office for the latest report. Tony was looking forward to giving it to him.

IAN WAS HELPING Sarah with a problem on a case, both of them completely consumed in their work when EJ's voice broke their concentration.

"Hey, Ian, gotta minute?"

Ian looked up, annoyed at first, then he caught his

friend's eye. They'd been friends—and partners—for so many years now that they could read each other's signals almost without trying. Sage teased him that EJ was his "work spouse."

It was clear that EJ had something urgent to tell him, and for whatever reason, he didn't want Sarah in on it—which in itself was odd. The three had rarely had reason to keep any secrets from one another. Sarah appeared to think so, too.

"We're busy here, in case you didn't notice. Wait your turn."

"Yeah, sorry about that." He swung his gaze to Ian again. "I just need your ear for a second. I have to go soon, or I wouldn't interrupt."

"Sure."

When Sarah started to object, and pushed her chair back with the obvious intention of joining them, EJ just smiled and cocked an eyebrow.

"Uh, you can just stay right there, young lady."

Her blue eyes flared as they met his teasing green ones, and his tone was teasing, too, so she backed off.

"If you guys are up to some surprise party nonsense for my birthday next week, well, okay. You could be a little more discreet about it, though. And make sure you bang heads with Logan on it, too."

EJ laughed and just winked, leading Ian back to his own office, where he closed the door and went to the computer, pulling up a file.

"I got this a few minutes ago," EJ announced with no further preamble.

Ian walked around the desk and looked—there was a picture of EJ's son, playing at the park.

"Nice picture, but what's the urgency?"

"It's from Jennie."

"What's going on, EJ?"

"She sent this from someone else's e-mail, with a stego-encoded message in the photo. It was something I taught her to do a while back. See the subject line?"

Ian read it; it said only "Fifth time sending this" and then the message above the photo simply said "I hope you get it."

"She's repeating a phrase we used when I was teaching her about simple stego-encoding, using the unused bits of information in graphics to bury messages."

"I know what stego is, EJ—why is this important? Why is she using someone else's e-mail?"

"It's a spoof account—she must have set up a fake one at a public server, and used it to send this. I tried to trace it, it may take a while—she covered her tracks pretty well. Here's the uncoded message."

EJ clicked on another screen, and hit Print. Ian took the printed message handed to him, and when he looked back up from reading, his gray eyes were like ice chips.

"Where's Reilly?"

"Don't know. Haven't seen him, haven't heard from him since the meeting yesterday."

"Did we try his cell?"

EJ looked at him as if he'd sprouted a horn from his head. "Yeah. First thing. No go. I've left a dozen messages. He must have turned it off or left it behind, or he's just not answering."

"Shit."

"Make that a double. If what she says is true…"

Ian shook his head. "There's no way Nate's dirty, or working for her family. If he was, I'd have known it."

"Something spooked her, and spooked her big-time, Ian. Jennie wouldn't take off like this, not unless she was seriously threatened."

"Agreed. Why not come to us? We could have helped her."

EJ shrugged. "If these guys found her again after so long, her first instinct would be to disappear. And if she thinks Nate's dirty, how could she know who to trust?"

Ian indicated the e-mail. "She trusts you, apparently."

"That was risky for her, considering. She's trying to protect us."

"From Nate? Jesus." Ian ran a hand over his face, thinking of the next step. "We need to find him, and we need to find out what's going on, *now*."

EJ looked Ian in the eye. "Playing devil's advocate, do you think there's a chance in hell she's right, and he's dirty?"

"I guess we can't be one hundred percent sure. Jennie's not prone to panicking for no reason."

Ian continued to study the message. "It's likely he took off after her. What the hell is going on?" His hand landed hard on the desk in frustration. He hated when things were out of control, especially when it meant the lives of his unit—of his friends—were endangered. Ian gazed out at the outer office where Nolan Wagner sat engrossed in his work.

"But he knows something."

"You think?"

"They're pals. Nathan picked him up last night. If you were in trouble, and if you didn't want anyone you worked with to know, who better to tell than an old friend?"

"An old friend with skills that might just come in handy when you were looking for someone who skipped town?" EJ added.

"Bingo."

"It's worth a shot," Ian agreed, wondering how he was going to handle it if they were right. They had no influence over what Nolan Wagner did—he was only working for them in a temporary capacity.

"I'll talk to him." EJ stepped forward, his soft Southern accent threaded with pure steel.

"You sure?"

EJ was already out the door, interrupting Nolan, whom Ian had found to be a deceptively sharp guy. His brain seemed to be working on several levels simultaneously, and yet he had a low-key personality. A guy Ian liked a lot and wouldn't balk at hiring—

depending on the part he might have played in this mess, if any.

EJ stood, hands on hips, talking to Nolan, who seemed to be talking a little too much for someone who didn't know anything. Ian walked out of the office, toward the two men. Luckily, Sarah had stepped out for the moment. He cut into their conversation, getting to the point quickly.

"You helped Nathan find Jennie?"

"I did."

"Why?"

"He asked me to."

"You didn't think this should have been brought to my attention?"

"Nathan didn't want you to know. He told me to keep it between us. Seeing as you asked…I figure the cat is out of the bag."

"That much is obvious!" Ian was furious at Nolan's interference, at this stranger getting in between him and his people.

"What the hell is going on, EJ?"

"Nathan had reason for not contacting us. It's not because he's a dirty cop. It's because he was supposedly investigating dirty cops."

"What? Who?"

"Us, apparently. Nate isn't working for the mob. He's working for IA. They were investigating Jennie, suspected she was a mole. And I guess they thought we could be involved, as well."

Ian let that set in for a moment, then pinned Nolan with a sharp look.

"I want to know everything you know."

"No problem."

NATHAN'S FINGERS WERE NUMB. He'd been walking around all day in just his leather jacket and jeans, and the weather was nasty. Still he kept going; he'd gotten to Lancaster early that morning and had been canvassing the place on foot, showing Jennie's picture at every hotel, B and B, but so far no luck.

He had to warm up; the diner looked inviting. It would be dark soon, and he was no closer to finding Jennie than when he arrived here. It could have been a red herring, a diversion, he realized. She could have purchased several tickets, intending to confuse. She could be somewhere else entirely.

He passed by the counter where several waitresses had congregated. Business was slow, and two were chatting while the third counted and split tips. He ordered coffee and the older waitress nodded and left her conversation to get his order.

As she approached, he reached into his pocket for his wallet, making sure he had enough cash on him for dinner. He was starving; he hadn't taken time for food since sometime yesterday.

When he pulled the wallet out, the picture of Jennie he'd been showing around fell to the floor. He reached for it—might as well show it around here, while he was sitting—but the waitress bent and picked it up first, looking at it before she handed it to him, then looking at it again.

"Is this your girl, hon? I daresay she looks just like Camille. Though the hair is all wrong."

The waitress smiled at him, put the coffee down on the table and stood poised to take his order, pen and pad in hand.

Nathan's pulse skyrocketed, and his sluggishness disappeared as he realized he might have finally found someone who could lead him to Jennie. He had to play it cool; she'd talk more if he followed the train of conversation she'd started.

"That's my girlfriend, but her name is Jennie."

"Spitting image of Camille, without the red hair, though. They say everyone has a twin—I've always pitied mine," The waitress, whose name tag identified her as Angie laughed at her own joke. "Can I take your order, hon?"

"BLT club and fries. Have you been friends with Camille for a long time?"

"Oh, goodness no. She just came in yesterday, and she's staying with a friend of mine. Just passing through. I just couldn't help noticing how much she resembled your girlfriend. They could be sisters. Lucky you."

She smiled again, and he smiled back—lucky him, indeed. Nathan did all he could to keep from jumping out of the chair.

"You say she's staying somewhere local? I can't find a room I can afford. Any chance I could find a room at the same inn?"

"Sorry, hon. Marge Sawyer doesn't run an inn, she's just helping out a friend. I can make some other recommendations, though, if you want to just wait a minute so I can get your order in."

"Would you have a phone book I could look at, Angie?" He smiled the smile his mother said could charm the green off of a tree. "I could call around to a few places, maybe, keep me from having to walk around in the cold."

"Absolutely, hon. It's freezing out there. Just a sec."

It was all Nathan could do to stay in his seat. He didn't want his food any longer; he wanted to find out where Marge Sawyer lived and find Jennie before she disappeared again. He had to appear calm. If he acted strangely that would tip the waitress off and she might call her friend and warn Jennie—*Camille.*

Angie came back with his food, and the phone book. His cell phone was lying on the counter, so he could make a show of calling places, though he wasn't wasting any more time than he had to. He grimaced at the small screen—messages were stacking up. He listened through them: EJ, wondering where the hell he was. He couldn't tell them; not yet.

He ate without tasting, finding Marge Sawyer's address. He memorized it, stood and left half his food behind uneaten. Throwing bills on the table, he got up to go, and just waved and smiled when Angie followed him out of the door, yelling after him that he'd left too much. He kept moving, knowing Jennie was only a few miles away.

8

MARGE HAD A LATE-NIGHT class on Tuesdays, so Jennie had caught a bus back to the farmhouse, arriving well after dark. She'd spent all day in the library and had contacted EJ, which had taken some time to manage. She'd hoped that she'd sent a message which wouldn't look suspicious to anyone but him.

He'd taught her that the code she used could only be read if the person you were sending it to knew the key. While he'd get the message, he wouldn't be able to find her. She'd erased the temporary e-mail she'd created from the student's account. As an extra measure, she'd disabled the original account, as well. She'd contacted campus security, posing as the student and asking that the account be wiped and reissued. It would be an inconvenience to the poor student, nevertheless it was her life on the line and she couldn't worry about things like that. No one should be able to trace back to it now.

She planned to leave tomorrow or the next day for the airport in Philly where she would leave the country. She would go to London first and work from there. Fortunately, she'd included a very authentic passport in her fake identity paperwork. Maybe she'd stay in London—lose herself in the crowds, rebuild her life as Camille Jackson. Or maybe she'd move on to somewhere even farther away, where she could really become lost, like New Zealand or Japan—then, finally, she could feel safe.

At the moment, her challenge was to find the extra key Marge had told her was left in the bucket of fake flowers in the southern corner of the porch. She stuck her hand in the bucket, feeling underneath the stiff plastic flowers.

"Jennie." Then, *"Maria."*

Reeling, she threw the bucket sideways. She knew the voice, had heard the same soft tone whispered across a pillow in the dark. She turned, jumping to her feet and squinting in the dark. She could tell by his profile; she could tell by his scent. It was Nathan.

He'd found her, and her blood ran cold. He stood in front of her, barring her way back across the porch. When it came to fight or flight, she still put her money on flight, and turned without saying a word, vaulting over the porch railing and taking off across the frozen fields.

"Jennie! Jennie, wait!"

Nathan took chase, jumping the rail, as well, and she could hear him crunching over the frost-covered, cut cornfields behind her. Panic blinded her—where was she running to? Where could she go? There was no neighbor close enough, no one home at the farm, and she had no vehicle to run to. She heard him calling behind her; she had to stop and face him. Even if it was the last thing she ever did, which it just might be.

He could outrun her, and at his pace, he would have overtaken her anyway. She had no choice. She had to confront him. Her eyes wandered toward the road, wondering if anyone passing by might see them and help, however, it was too dark.

He stopped short, breathing hard.

"Nathan. If that's even your name. How did you find me?"

"I had help."

She barked out a laugh. "I bet you did. How long have you worked for my uncle? From the very beginning or did they employ you just recently, after you joined the unit?"

There was a pause, and she waited, her heart pounding so hard she could barely hear her own thoughts. His response sounded as if he didn't know what she was talking about. Right.

"What? Jennie…listen, no. I don't know your uncle. I mean, I know who he is—"

"And who I am," she spat out the words accusingly.

"Yes. I know who you are. That's true. What I don't know is why you ran. You have to explain that to me."

"You've *got* to be kidding. I found out about *you*, too, Nathan. I know why you were after me. I know why you were so interested in me. Have you had fun with your little cat-and-mouse game? How long did you plan to drag this out, Nathan? How long before you were going to finish it, or were you waiting on my uncle so he could have the honors?"

"Jennie, I don't know why you seem to think I'm in contact with your uncle. There are definitely some wires crossed here, and we have to figure out what's going on."

Confusion tangled her thoughts. What was he saying? Why didn't he just kill her as he'd come here to do? As he'd intended on doing all along? Why did he sound so reasonable? Jennie's heart urged her to listen to him, however her instincts told her to survive. Caught in between she could only ask one question.

"So you aren't here to kill me?"

She could feel his astonishment arc across the dark space that separated them. Then he stepped forward again, and his voice was low, controlled and deadly serious.

"Kill you? Hell, no. I'm here to arrest you."

"ARREST ME? Arrest me for *what?*"

Nathan's heart skipped at hearing exactly what he wanted to hear. The question, the indignity and outrage in her voice, encouraged him. He wanted to draw her out a little more, though, hoping they wouldn't both freeze to death in the process.

"You said you knew all about me. Why I was investigating you."

"Investigating me? For what?"

"You need to stop repeating everything I say, and answer the question, Jen. I'm willing to hear your side of the story. One way or the other, I'm taking you back to Norfolk, and we're going to clear this up. If you're what they say you are, you're going to face the music. I'll make sure of that, you can count on it."

He meant it.

"I want to know, Jennie," Nathan rasped, his teeth chattering in the cold. "Are you a mole, infiltrating the department through the Witness Protection Program? Have you been feeding inside information to your family all this time? And are Ian and EJ in on it?"

She fell back several steps, and he pulled his gun out of reflex, intent on stopping her if she was going to run. Why would she run unless she was guilty of the charges he leveled at her?

"Nathan, you can't possibly think…who would think such a thing…?"

"I don't know what to think, Jennie. You said you'd found out about me, about my investigation. Unless you were guilty, why would you run?"

"What investigation? I thought you were working with my uncle, Nathan. I thought you were sent by them to find me, maybe to kill me or just to keep track of me until they decided what to do with me."

"Why on earth would you think that?"

"I found a disc in your dresser—it had all the files of everyone in the family there, all the known contacts, all their information. You know all about me, you admitted that. What else was I to think? There's no other way you could know all that, except through them, or EJ and Ian—and they wouldn't have ever told you. They never told their wives, they never even told Sarah."

"They didn't tell me, Jen. I'm not working for your uncle."

"Who then?"

If he expected her to come clean, he had to, as well.

"IA—internal affairs. They got word on you from the feds, a lead that suggested you were feeding information back to your family. Your uncle's associates avoided some charges because they received information on raids that only people at certain levels of law enforcement—like us— would know about."

"*Jesus and Mary,* Nathan—"

He cut her off. "How did you manage to live so successfully all these years? With all of your uncle's resources, how could they not find you? And then your brother was tracked here. A month ago he came to Norfolk. IA assumed it was to see you, to make contact, and that initiated the investigation. They felt they had enough to look deeper. If Tony was here, and you weren't dead, then there must be some other explanation—some other reason behind it. Were they right?"

"Tony? Tony came to Norfolk?"

"You didn't know that?"

"No!" she yelled, holding her hands to either side of her head, and Nathan backed off a step.

"I didn't know that! If I'd known that I would have been gone! Tony works for my uncle, Nathan. If they found me, why didn't they come after me? What the hell is going on?"

"That's exactly the question we both need an answer to. So you're not working with them?"

"No. I am *not* working with my uncle. Are you nuts? Are the federal government and all of the idiots in IA completely insane? Do you think my uncle would ever cut a deal with me? Do you think he would ever let me live, considering what I did to him? I'm not a mole, I swear it. They could get any number of people inside to give them that kind of information—why would I be spared to do it?"

Nathan waited three beats, digesting what she said. He wanted so badly to believe her. He analyzed her reactions, her responses, from every vantage point, and his gut urged him to take a risk. He would still bring her back to Norfolk—regardless of the situation, it would be the safest place for her. She took several steps closer, and he prepared for any move she might be tempted to make to disarm him. Instead she just stood there.

"Please, Nathan. I believe you, that you're not working for my uncle. That you are working for IA. It makes sense. Can you see that this makes sense, too? That I wouldn't do such a thing? I would never endanger my friends, and their families like that. And, no, EJ and Ian are the best cops on the force—to say they're dirty, to even imply it—is a slap in the face. Whoever said it should be out of a job."

Her words were so sincere, he felt himself wavering. It was probably the cold, the exhaustion or that he just wanted what she was saying to be true, still he believed her. Lowering his gun, he didn't put it away, not yet.

"You have to go back, Jennie. You have to let them know you aren't dirty. And we have to find out why your brother was in Norfolk."

"If I'm not dead now, he didn't find me. He might have been looking. He couldn't have found me. It's too close, that's for sure. That's all I know. I can't go back, I just can't, Nathan. It could be a trap, it could endanger everyone. You, too. This could all be a trap."

He relented, shoving his gun back under his jacket.

"You think the information was a plant, meant to flush you out? To use the very program and people who protected you to show them where you were?"

She nodded. "Most likely. There are all kinds of bad cops linked up with the mob. It wouldn't take much. I'm surprised they didn't think of it sooner. It's clever, really."

"We can't know who's in on it—could even be one of the IA guys. Maybe that's why they were so insistent that EJ and Ian not know. They'd know this was full of shit."

"So you see why I can't go back."

"Damn."

"Yes." She sounded shaken from emotion, or from the cold. "Thank you."

"For what?"

"Taking a chance on believing me. And for not shooting me." Her voice, incredibly, held a hint of humor, and he smiled in spite of everything.

"We have to decide what to do next."

"You should go. Let me disappear."

"No way, Jen. Not happening."

"It's really the only way, Nathan."

He stepped forward, closing the distance between them.

"Whatever's going on, we're going to face it. EJ and Ian could still be in danger—and no one uses me like this. If that's what happened, I'm going to find out who, and I'm going to find out why. And we need somewhere safe to be until I do."

"I contacted EJ," she blurted.

"When? How?"

"I sent him a coded message. I ditched my cell phone, figuring they had it tagged, and I bought a temp one. I hacked into an e-mail account at the local college today and sent him a stego-encoded message. I...um..."

"What?"

She blew out a heavy sigh. "I told them you were dirty. I told them I ran because of what I found in your apartment."

Nathan was stunned for a moment, and then, caught off guard by the insanity of it all, he laughed. And then he laughed harder, until he was bent over double, needing to catch his breath.

"Nathan? Are you all right?"

"Oh, man." He straightened, catching his breath. "Ian is *so* going to kick my ass when we get back. I guess we need to talk to them. From a distance, preferably."

"We can't let anyone know where we are—we don't know who's watching who anymore."

"True. Let's go somewhere to get warm and talk about it. We'll get a plan in place, and see what happens."

She nodded, heading to the house they'd run away from, and he fell into pace beside her. He hoped Marge didn't mind a second guest.

"WE'VE FOUND THEM, UNCLE."

Tony looked his uncle in the eye, cool as a cucumber though he was so tense his chest felt as if there was a metal band around it. Informing Bruno of Jennie's whereabouts was a wild card—he had to play this shrewdly, or it could turn very, very wrong.

His uncle's eyes drew to slits as he put down the book he'd been reading.

"Where?"

"She's in Pennsylvania with her cop boyfriend—she caught a whiff of something, took off and he took off after her. So we have him on the radar, and visual confirmation that he's been showing her picture around, and a little inside information that our Maria hasn't shown up for work for two days. I think it's a safe bet."

"Send Joe to check it out."

Tony squared his shoulders—this was the hard part.

"With all due respect, Uncle, this is my sister. She betrayed all of us, left my mother alone, sent you to prison. If anyone goes, it should be me."

Bruno sat back, studying him carefully.

"You could kill your own blood?"

Tony didn't drop his stare, but let a tight, hard smile form. "Of course. You did."

His uncle didn't respond to the bold statement at first, then he laughed, seemingly finding it acceptable. Tony wanted to slit his throat on the spot for the fact that he could laugh over killing his own family. Tony's father.

"Good enough. You go. Only to confirm it's her, and make sure she doesn't run again. When I get word from you, I'll be there. I want to do it." Tony watched his uncle's pupils widen with anticipation. "I want mine to be the last face that bitch sees."

"And the cop?"

His uncle shrugged, picking up his book again. "Do whatever you want with him. Just leave her for me."

JENNIE TOOK HER TIME building the fire. She heard the shower running upstairs as Nathan cleaned up, and hoped against hope that Marge wouldn't end up walking in the door. Both of them would be out on their backsides in the cold if her new host thought she was bringing strange men home. Marge was so trusting. A really nice, solid person, Jennie thought. The kind of person she'd rarely come across in her life.

Her family life had always been lively, full of boisterous personalities and tempers flaring. Her life since then, at least on a professional level, hadn't been much different. Being here in Marge's farmhouse, with all of the Sawyer family's notions surrounding her, and thinking about how...*stable*... Marge was, even in the face of her terrible breakup, was making Jennie acknowledge how she needed more of that in her life.

Maybe if she lived through this, she'd find it.

The cedar was crackling and filled the room with the best scents possible. Except for food. Jennie's stomach rumbled. Marge had invited her to use whatever was on hand, and she was going to take her up on the offer.

The shower stopped, and she found her heart thudding hard at the thought of Nathan walking down those stairs. Everything she believed was true had shifted, and now she had to adjust.

She still had to leave, no matter what Nathan thought. The fact was that if Tony had been spotted in Norfolk, then the mob was closing in on her. There was just no other explanation.

It was the kind of information that normally would have crossed her desk—she kept informed of all mob sightings and activities, information that she inputted into her databases and mapped for criminal analysis. Someone had known and had made sure she didn't.

That meant there was someone dirty on the inside. Even if they found out who, her cover was blown. It would be impossible for her to resume her old life.

She walked into the kitchen as she heard Nathan's footsteps hit the top stair, needing to avoid him for just a few minutes longer. He'd read her far too easily if she didn't have time to regroup.

"Hey, where'd you get to?" he called out, and she swallowed, clearing her throat.

"I'm out here, in the kitchen."

Striving for composure, she opened the freezer and foraged for whatever she could cobble together for supper.

Then he was there. His fresh, manly scent filled the air around her, and she felt his presence like a thunderbolt. She couldn't breathe for a second, and stilled as she reached for a package of frozen chicken, her hand drawing slowly out of the freezer.

"This place is beautiful. It reminds me a little of my relatives' houses in Ireland, though theirs were much smaller. The sense of homeyness and comfort is the same. I'd love to have a place like this someday."

"Me, too. I've admired all of the handwork. I wish I had time to learn." She hadn't intended to sound so wistful, and faced the sink to work on thawing out the meat. She turned on the faucet, and was startled when Nathan came up behind her, cupping her shoulders. Water splashed everywhere as it came out of the faucet too hard, and she reached to turn it off, relieved he'd backed off, as well.

"Sorry, hon. Didn't mean to startle you."

Closing her eyes, she knew she had to deal with this. Turning, she faced him, ruthlessly closing her heart to the warmth she found in his gaze.

"I'm sorry, too. I didn't mean to jump like that. This is all going too fast, and we have no idea what's going to happen. No more than a few hours ago, I thought you were going to kill me. A day or so before that I thought you…"

She stopped, unwilling to finish. He came closer, crowding her, making it more difficult, as if that were possible.

"You thought I was what?"

"It doesn't matter now."

His brow furrowed as he regarded her carefully, and reached forward to grasp her ice-cold hands.

"You're cold."

"It's just from rummaging through the freezer."

"Hmm." He appeared pensive, as if he was making a decision about something, and she waited, not having anything to say for herself—or not knowing what she should say.

"I can tell you what I was thinking about you before this all happened," he said, finally breaking the silence. He tipped her chin up, locked her gaze onto his. "I was thinking about a future with the only woman who's ever really grabbed my heart. I was thinking about all the years ahead of us, because I was so crazy about you after just a few weeks I couldn't imagine my life without you."

"Nathan, this isn't—"

"Ah." He held his finger to her lips, and the touch nearly undid her. It certainly stopped whatever she'd been about to say. "This is my turn. You had yours. I'm telling you how I felt, and how I still feel. We just have to get to the other side of this. And we will."

She wrenched her hands away, walking across the kitchen, afraid to hope.

"Nathan, you know that's impossible. It means leaving everything and everyone you know behind, forever. And let me tell you, that's not a way to live."

"And yet it's what you were about to do. Again."

"*I* have no choice. I'm grateful to know that you hadn't betrayed me—well, not in the way I thought, anyway." She saw him flinch at that, and didn't waver. He had lied to her, investigated her, thought the worst of her. She couldn't forget that. "None of that matters in the long run. I'm still living with a target on my back, and my identity has been compromised. I can't go back to my former life—ever."

"The way I see it, we were both lying."

"I had reason."

"And I didn't?"

He shook his head, and she backed off of that argument. There was no winner on that score. He was right; she had lied. To save her life. And he'd been doing his duty, which seemed shallow in comparison.

"Well, it's all out in the open now. EJ and Ian—"

"Can't do one damned thing about it," she finished for him. "No one can protect me except for me. Hell, Nathan, think about it. Think about what they did, how they managed to get inside, to turn my own department against me, in order to flush me out. Do you think there's anywhere I could be safe? Do you think any of my friends could be safe? You?"

He just stared at her, soaking it in, and not liking what he was hearing, she could tell.

"They would find you, and they would get to me through you. Or people I love would get caught in the cross fire because they were part of my life, and so they'd have to be wiped out. This man…he killed his own brother and nephew, Nathan, my father and brother. Do you understand that kind of evil? There's no way you can, believe me."

She hadn't been aware that tears had started

staining her face, choking her voice. Nathan crossed the kitchen and gently pulled her up close.

"Sorry, babe. You're stuck with me now. We're going to figure this out."

"You—"

She was cut off by the loud jangling of the phone. She'd been using a cell phone primarily for so many years she'd almost forgotten what the sound was like, and it shook her frayed nerves.

"I'll get that. It could be Marge."

He nodded, releasing her. She went over to the phone, thankful for any reprieve.

It was Marge, apparently, and Nathan listened to Jennie "mmm" and "sure" and "uh-huh, no problem" with her back turned to him.

Restless, he took the chicken from the sink, grabbing a frying pan and some frozen veggies to occupy himself while she talked. Finally, she hung up. He floured the chicken, placing it in some butter he'd melted and thrown a few herbs into. Within seconds the delicious aroma permeated the kitchen.

"So how is ol' Marge?" he asked conversationally about the woman he'd never met, trying to lighten the mood.

"She's fine. She won't be home tonight. She's conducting a last-minute study group, and is just going to stay on campus. She didn't want me to worry."

"Works out conveniently for us, huh?"

"Yeah, I guess." She stood over the stove, appreciating his culinary skill, lifting the lid on the veggies to check them. "You didn't have to do that. Thanks."

"I like to cook, and I'm starving."

"We agree there."

He flipped the chicken, and turned the heat down.

"Listen, Jennie, or…" He looked at her intently, wondering if he should say his next thought out loud.

"What?"

"Should I call you by your real name? It suits you so much more than Jennie, and I've always thought of you as Maria, since I found out."

The sadness he saw in her face made him wish he hadn't said it.

"I can't ever use that name again, Nathan, not even in private. I have to become who I am, even in the most…personal ways."

She wasn't ready to accept yet that this was all going to change. He knew she was right, on one level. Yet he was determined to find a way. He also knew she wouldn't really be receptive to him pushing the point at the moment, so they had to find something else to talk about—for now.

He picked up the fillets of chicken while she scooped out the veggies and dotted them with butter. They worked naturally as a team even when they were at odds. The thought inspired hope; things were going to work out.

Placing the food on Marge's sturdy kitchen table where there was some leftover bread and a half-gone bottle of wine, they ate in silence. Then Nathan decided to bring up the other difficult topic they had to talk about.

"We should call Ian and EJ as soon as we can."

She nodded hesitantly. "We can't use Marge's phone, and I really don't want to use mine."

"No problem. We can use mine. They've been after me all day from what I can tell from the messages piled up."

One of her eyebrows arched high. "You mean you didn't shut it off?"

He shook his head, swallowing another bite of chicken. "No, I couldn't risk missing a call from you, and EJ and Ian wouldn't have known anything about me until today, so they wouldn't have been bothering."

"How did you find me, anyway, if I might ask?"

He grinned. "So you can make sure not to make the same mistake next time?"

"Live and learn."

"Well, I had help, as I said. For one thing, IA had you under surveillance—it appears Norris didn't exactly trust me entirely, so he had someone else watching you. They lost you on your way downtown. I had a rough idea, though, where you might have been heading."

"Chad Norris?"

"Yeah, why?"

"Nothing much. He asked me out about fifty times when I started working in Norfolk. Real pain in the backside. I finally had to be unmistakably rude to get him to lay off."

Nathan grinned again, wider, finding so much satisfaction in that little tidbit of information.

"He's a jerk. Though I can't see him being dirty. And he knew where you were all along, so if he was the source of the leak, they wouldn't have assigned me to anything."

"That makes sense."

Nathan watched Jennie sip her wine, and followed the path of the sparkling, golden liquid as it passed her cherry lips and moved over her tongue. Desire coiled in his belly, and it took him a few moments to regain his concentration.

"So, yes…we'll call them when we're done here. They'll be glad to know you're safe."

"So how'd you find out what bus I was on?"

"Oh, right." He'd lost complete track of what they'd been talking about, and still was having trouble concentrating as he thought about sweeping his tongue down the velvet skin of her neck.

"My old friend, Nolan Wagner, helped me."

"*The* Nolan Wagner?"

"You know him?"

"Of course. At this point you know I was raised in Boston, as well—he was huge there, in the news all the time. Child genius, and then he was fired from his academic position, right?"

"It was more like he escaped. He was trapped in

that weird genius gig, and I hadn't seen him since he was a professor in one of my classes. He's like a new man. It freed him."

"Well, with brainpower like that, no surprise you could track me."

"Hey, I had something to do with it, too, you know. I was very determined."

The suggestion in his voice created the most beautiful rose blush in her skin, and he knew she wasn't immune to him.

"Anyway, I managed to finesse some information from the security office at the bus station—"

"You conned them in other words?"

"Social engineering, sweetheart. With that, we followed a path until Nolan managed to use some souped-up photo software he's been building to get information off the ticket you were holding at the counter, and we just connected the dots, and here I am."

"Very slick. I'm glad you're both on my side," she said, sounding amazed.

"I am. On your side. And I don't plan on leaving it."

"Nathan—"

He didn't let her finish, pulling his phone out of his pants pocket.

"How about we get this over with?"

9

Ian sat back in the deep leather chair of his study, listening to Nathan, who'd called him on his private line. He couldn't believe what he was hearing; then again, yes he could. HotWires cops falling in love and taking stupid chances was a repeated phenomenon in his office. Considering he himself had led the charge, doing exactly the same thing when he'd fallen in love with Sage, how could he fault Nathan?

Because he was the boss, that's why.

"I want to know where you are, Reilly."

"Sorry, Ian, no can do."

"I beg your pardon?" Ian said sharply, seconds away from completely losing his temper. He looked up when he felt his wife's hand on his shoulder. Sage was even more beautiful than ever. His pulse began to race for an entirely different reason.

"Patience," she mouthed to him.

"Okay, okay," he muttered, addressing her and Nathan both. "You'd better get her back here. It's where you'll be safest. I'll give you a day. Then we're coming after you both."

He should have already sent agents to track them down. They'd be able to find Nathan by his cell signal. He'd decided, though, to have Nathan handle it for the time being. If for no other reason than there could be someone watching them in Norfolk, and if Ian could find out where they were, others might, too. What a freakin' mess.

"Ian, I'm working on it. She's not exactly… agreeable."

"I've talked with Norris, and he wasn't happy to know the cat's out of the bag. To be fair, he's got Feds on his back—they want to know where she is, and they won't wait long. We've been stalling. You were smart to call me at home.

"Make sure Jennie knows that if she runs again, she'll be considered a fleeing felon. She needs to come back or she could end up in big trouble."

"I think she's much more worried about ending up dead."

Ian didn't have much response to that. The kid sounded tired. Ian believed Nathan could deal with the situation as long as he didn't let his emotions cloud his judgment, which Ian knew firsthand was easier said than done. However, Sage had often made the argument that being in love could make you see things more clearly; it helped you get your priorities straight. He hoped that was true for Nathan.

"She's in the shower at the moment. She's afraid

of endangering you all, Ian, and the kids. It's not just about her, you know that. It never was."

Ian wearily rubbed his hand over his face.

"I know. We have to do something by tomorrow. If we don't the Feds will. We know why she ran now, but it makes her look guilty. Up to that point they didn't have much of anything."

"It was my fault for leaving that disc where it could be found. In a way, I'm glad—at least things are out in the open now."

"There is something to that. For what it's worth, Nate, we know you were doing your job. I understand why you were doing what you did, and why you couldn't say anything. I don't like it, and I plan on having words with Norris once this is over. I do understand your part in it."

"Thanks. I hated being in that position, and I never believed it was true, not of Jennie, and certainly not of you and EJ." He cleared his throat, changing the subject, "Do you have any more news on why her brother was spotted in the city a few weeks ago? She didn't know, and when I told her, it really flipped her out. She's convinced they've found her."

"It seems like they've come close. I know surveillance was put on Tony Castone. They tried to tag him up in Boston, however he seems to have gone AWOL, fell off the map."

"Then he's off somewhere doing Bruno's dirty work. If they know about Jennie, they could be searching for her, too. I can keep her here. I don't know if I can get her back there, Ian, and I'm not even sure I want to."

"We'll cover as long as we can. Do what you have to, but don't let her out of your sight. I know you two have something, Nate. She means a lot to all of us here, too. Keep that in mind."

"I will, on all counts. We'll be in touch."

Ian placed the phone back in its holder, then gathered Sage close to him, looking past her to where their daughter, one of the twins, had fallen asleep in the big chair where Sage had been reading to her.

"Are they okay?" Sage's voice was soft as she ran her hand over his hair, soothing and exciting him at the same time.

"Yeah, for now. They have some hard days ahead of them. If she hadn't run…"

"You can hardly blame her."

With everything blowing up, and Nathan calling him at home—a call Sage had answered—Ian had come clean with Sage, had told her the secret he'd been holding for a long time about Jennie. Sage didn't seem all that surprised. She suspected that there was something.

"I can't blame her, still she has to come back."

"Nathan will find a way."

"How do you know?"

She looked at him, copper hair falling over her shoulders, grown long since the girls were born.

"Because he's in love with her, and love makes you find a way. After all, we did."

Ian drew her down next to him, covering her mouth with his, opting to believe that she was right.

NATHAN SHUT HIS PHONE OFF. Now that he'd made contact and found Jennie, there was no reason to keep it on, especially since the Feds would likely be tracking his signal. It was a good thing Ian had apparently bought them some time. Question was, what were they going to do now? They were in the dark—they didn't know how close Tony or Bruno Castone might be, or what the next move should be.

He and Jennie had gotten lucky with Marge not coming home for the night. They'd have to move on soon, by morning anyway. That gave them a long night alone in this house together. The thought had his heart racing. From upstairs, he heard the sound of Jennie's footsteps along the hall to her bedroom. He climbed the stairs to join her.

Her door wasn't completely shut, and he inhaled the scent of her shampoo as he opened it. She stood with her back to him beside an oval, freestanding mirror on the other side of the room, a towel slipped down around her waist as she applied lotion to her arms. She looked like one of those voluptuous women fresh out of the bath painted by Degas.

Her skin glowed softly in the twilight, her long hair was draped over one shoulder, covering the slope of her left breast while exposing the other to his view. She was lush and radiant, and felt himself harden. When she met his gaze in the mirror, there was a flicker of surprise, yet she didn't shy away. It was all the invitation he needed.

"Nathan, no," she sighed more than commanded as his hands slipped over her shoulders, moving along the delicate curves of her torso, then around to cup her breasts. Heaven couldn't feel this good.

Did she honestly think he would live his life without ever being able to touch her like this? He felt her quiver as he began stroking her delicate skin. He wanted to make sure she accepted what was happening between them. Meeting her brown eyes in the mirror—she'd ditched the contact lenses, thank God, because he loved her big brown eyes—he halted his caresses and spoke softly.

"Tell me to stop and I will—if it's what you really want. You have to mean it, Jen. Don't play with me, I can't take that."

She opened her mouth as if to speak, and his heart seized in his chest for a moment, thinking she really would tell him to stop.

"No, don't stop. Please," she whispered.

He had to pause for a moment, almost shuddering with relief as her words registered, and he buried his face in her neck, tasting her skin.

"I don't ever want to stop, honey. I don't think I could ever stop…."

She made a move to face him, the towel dropping so that she was nude before him. He murmured his dissent, as he held her in place, his hands on her hips.

"Just watch, Jen. Watch what we have together so you can see how we are, how amazing this is. You're incredible," he rasped as he drew a finger lightly up the length of her spine, delighting in the erotic arch of her body as she responded.

"That's it," he encouraged, determined to show her that there was no way either one of them was ever going to walk away from this if he had anything to say about it.

He couldn't keep his hands off the satiny skin of her breasts; he was obsessed with the velvety stiffness of her nipples as he rolled them between his fingers. Every touch was familiar and yet strikingly new—made sweeter by the fact that he'd almost lost her, that he hadn't known if he would ever be with her again, just this way. Regardless of what tomorrow brought, tonight they needed this, needed to rediscover each other, to share each other's strength.

Her soft gasps and sighs only further aroused him, and he snugged against her full bottom. For now, he was content to make love to her slowly, reacquainting himself with the details of her body. Like how she tasted of honey and vanilla, he thought as he dragged his tongue over her shoulder, and then down the length of her spine. He sank to the floor, drawing his palms down her front as he did so. He loved the subtle curve of her belly, the flare of her hip...and all the other spaces he had yet to explore.

Her head dropped back and she moaned when he widened her stance, placing his hands between her thighs so that she was fully visible to him. He ran his fingers over the dark nest of hair covering her sex, never once touching her exactly where he knew she needed to be touched. She was panting, hot feminine breaths that turned him on even more, and he watched her long, slender fingers clench into fists as she trembled beneath his touch.

He kissed the back of one knee, then the other, suckling the tender spot as he slid his hands up the inside of her taut thighs. Finally, slowly, he trailed one finger along the cleft of her luscious butt cheeks, all the way from the cute little dimple at the lower part of her back to her slick, swollen clit. She cried out his name, and he left a long, sucking kiss on the soft curve of her backside to let her know he loved hearing it.

He wanted more—he wanted to see everything she was feeling, not just hear it.

Nathan went over to the bed, which was already turned down, and patted it, indicating to her that he wanted her there. She'd turned to watch him, her face flushed with desire, her body ripe with it, then she did as he asked. His cock stiffened even more just looking at her, dying to find its home inside her hot, sweet body. He was determined to wait and do this right.

He heard her whisper his name in a question when he left her side, walked over to the mirror and lifted it up close to the bed. It was heavier than it looked, but it only took him a moment to position it. He met her curious gaze, smiling as he started taking his own clothes off.

"Do you trust me, Jen?"

She looked tentative at first, then nodded. Within seconds he was completely naked—and unabashedly aroused. Joining her on the bed, he ignored the mirror for the moment, drawing her next to him and groaning at the sensation of their skin touching from shoulder to toe. Unable to resist, he sank into the deep kiss she offered as she pressed against him.

Their kisses grew hungrier, hotter, and it seemed as if she was touching him everywhere, which was fine with him. When her hand slipped around his cock and squeezed, he knew he wouldn't last if he didn't slow things down again.

"Jennie, come here. Like this."

He placed her against the sturdy headboard, glancing up to make sure they were both visible in the mirror. Satisfied, he leaned down, capturing a nipple in his teeth, and slid his hands down to gently part her legs again so that when he turned his head, he could see everything in their reflection, and so could she.

"Jennie…watch…."

Sliding his hand down along her sex, he probed and explored, manipulating her glistening, silky folds as they watched, and was gratified when she groaned in excitement, nudging against him, asking for more.

He was happy to give it. He swept kisses over her stomach, then up along her shoulder as he loved her, sliding his hand intimately between her thighs, massaging the tender flesh in ways that had her arching and twisting beneath him. She was slick, hot and, oh, so close.

He rolled over, settling in between her thighs, applying his mouth to the area where his hand had been, and almost came when she screamed in release. He couldn't see, but he could imagine the picture they made in the mirror.

"Don't move. I want you to come for me again, baby."

Taking her hand in his, he caught the glimmer of apprehension in her expression, though it lasted only a second.

Twining their fingers, he moved her hand over her crotch, reminding her to be still as the excitement built again for them both, and slowly, purposefully, he slid their twined fingers, two of his wrapped around one of hers, inside of her. She trembled, shifting slightly to accommodate the position, whimpering softly when he thrust deeper.

Nathan was sure he'd never seen anything as erotic in his life as he rotated his thumb so that it brushed her engorged clit. He was deeply gratified, as if he'd been handed a precious gift when she'd lost all sense of self-consciousness and brought her legs up, squeezing so hard as she came that he couldn't move his hand, or hers, for a moment. She was flushed with pleasure, her breath catching as she tried to speak.

"Nathan, that was—"

"I know. I saw."

Trembling with his own pent up desire, he couldn't wait any longer. Kissing her deeply, he rubbed his aching erection against her silky thigh, feeling her pulse pound as he framed her face.

"I need you, Jen. I think I've always needed you. But I need you now almost more than ever."

His words touched her, the boundaries she'd so carefully constructed tumbling down with hardly a fight. Opening herself to him had felt right, so natural and good, as it had from the first time he'd ever kissed her.

Everything he did to her, with her, was perfect, and she felt tears gather. She was lost and scared and totally in love. For the moment, she focused on the hot kisses he was sharing with her, trying not to let the rest overwhelm her.

"I need you, too, Nathan. I want to see you—I love watching what we do to each other."

She knew just how to make that happen. Shifting away from those seductive kisses, difficult as it was, she shimmied down and flipped over, getting on all fours facing the mirror. Nathan was behind her, his skin ruddy with desire, his eyes blazing with need and realization of what she wanted.

He positioned himself behind her, grasping her hips and planting such heated kisses on her back that she moaned just from the touch of his lips and tongue. He set her on fire as no other man had ever done; she'd always known she had a passionate nature, but she'd never explored it. With Nathan, she wanted to experience it all.

She bit her lip, looking into the mirror. Her own visage stunned her—the desire and the naked need she displayed shaking her to the core. She needed him desperately, nudging against him suggestively, but he didn't penetrate her as she expected. Instead, he slid the solid length of his erection along her slippery cleft, creating such intense sensations. Shuddering, she pushed back, seeking him more insistently.

"Nathan, *I need you,*" she ground out between clenched teeth, biting back the more emotional words she'd almost spoken instead, making sure he knew he didn't have to wait for her. She was ready, hell, she was going to melt into a puddle if he didn't take her soon.

The flames only jumped higher rather than being extinguished as he prodded at her opening with his cock, teasing her until she knotted her fingers into the quilt and almost begged, her words no more than a whimper.

She was too needy to be surprised at the sight of the feral, raw desire in her expression, reflected back at her as she watched him poised behind her, torturing her to the very last second. The image before her blurred as he slid in deep, filling her and growling his pleasure loudly. His fingers clasped the flesh of her backside as he pushed in, then drew out so slowly she almost died with the sheer sensation of it.

She made herself keep her eyes open in spite of the thrill of pleasure she wanted to lose herself in, and watched him—the wonder and almost painful pleasure evident on his face. The tension in his jaw, the proud angle of his chin as he fought for control.

Satisfaction at her effect on him had her wanting to surprise him, to really push him to the edge. Balancing carefully, she lifted up, bringing her back up to his chest, shifting so that she could fit his thick cock even more tightly inside.

Her name burst from his lips as he thrust upward, his hands circling her for balance as much as closeness, covering her breasts and holding there until he steadied into the new position. He pumped upwards, finding the right rhythm. He felt so good, so thick and hot inside of her, she never wanted it to end. She also wanted to make him crazy—to seduce him even as much as she was being seduced.

She covered his hands with hers as he kneaded her breasts. Dipping her chin, she pushed her breasts up until she could flick out her tongue against the tips, catching his knuckles as she did so, and eliciting such a hot comment from him that she felt wicked and beautiful and did it again.

Together, they watched their erotic joining, the evidence of their connection and the magic they brought each other undeniable as their raspy breathing. They seemed to be fighting the pleasure as well as urging each other forward, denying the ultimate end of a moment they didn't want to let go of, and yet pushed closer and closer to the end by the surging demands of their bodies.

Jennie's pleasure was peaking. She needed him to open himself to her as much as she had for him. He was more than willing. A shiver of something beyond desire rippled through her as she saw his eyes turn so dark with arousal they appeared almost black. He looked dangerous, and she loved that she could bring this wildness out in him.

He pushed forward, releasing his hold on her and returning her to her original position. Free to move as he needed to, he gripped her hips once more, his fingers teasing sensitive spots as he picked up speed, thrusting into her urgently, hammering deeper, harder, faster, until Jennie's body felt like one long flame of pleasure.

As he climaxed, he threw his head back, victorious and gloriously defeated all at once, fucking her with such complete abandon that she came in a whirling vortex of pleasure, trusting him to hang on as she tumbled over the edge once more.

He collapsed over her, both of their bodies limp and slick, then wrapped his arms around her, as if he were unwilling to endure any space between them.

In that most exposed moment, where her body, her heart and her soul were painfully open to him, he said what she'd imagined hearing a million times. As he covered her mouth in a tender kiss, he whispered her name reverently: *Maria.*

TONY BLINKED, trying to stretch as he woke up, ending up, though, slamming his elbow and his knee into the center console and steering wheel as he did so. Disoriented, he bolted upright, knocking the cold cup of coffee resting in the curve of the steering wheel onto his lap.

"Damn! Shit!" He swore, picking up the cup and searching for something to blot the coffee from his lap. He hadn't meant to fall asleep—he'd tracked Reilly to town and followed him here. To where he'd waited in the dark for Maria to appear. As she had.

Since they'd arrived, Tony kept watch, making sure he was the only one who knew where they were—he couldn't take any chances since his uncle could be running a double game behind his back. Anxiety gripped him as he figured out how long he'd been sleeping—checking his watch he saw that only an hour had passed. Everything was probably fine. He'd feel better if he'd managed to stay awake.

Tony remembered seeing them on the porch. Maria hadn't been glad when Reilly had showed up, that's for sure. She didn't want anyone to find her—

not even her lover, by the looks of it. Tony wasn't quite sure what to make of that, and it worried him.

She'd seemed frightened, too, and it'd been all Tony could do to stay put; he didn't like seeing his sister being chased. He smiled to himself, remembering how Maria had always been able to take care of herself. She was one tough cookie and she'd reminded him and Gino frequently that she didn't need her brothers saving her.

In fact, with Gino, it had often been the other way around, Tony and Maria both had their turns rescuing their younger sibling. Gino had been a more gentle soul—much to their father's disappointment. Gino was easygoing, still he hadn't dealt with confrontation well, and when he was a kid his big mouth had gotten him in his share of trouble.

Tony felt the stab of emptiness that always hit when he thought about his dead brother. Maria had done her part to try to make things right; now it was his turn.

He turned his thoughts back to his sister and Reilly. Maybe they'd just had a fight. It looked like Reilly had won, which was no small feat, if Maria's temper was as hot as it had always been. Tony was stalling before he would call his uncle and let them know he'd "found" her. He had to make sure all of the pieces were in place.

So, he'd cut the engine, and only started the car for heat intermittently, camping out behind a closed vegetable stand across the road from where Maria was staying. How did she come to be here? Was it her home? Did it belong to a friend? They seemed to be there alone. Tony would be getting that information soon enough. His fed contacts were checking the place out, and would arrive as soon as Tony confirmed contact with Bruno.

Wanting to make sure his sister was okay, Tony had risked leaving his spot to cross to the windows after she and Reilly had gone inside. He'd told himself it was surveillance, but he really just wanted to reassure himself that everything was going to work out.

Tony wasn't crazy about the hair color Maria had changed to. At least it did make her more difficult to pick out of a crowd. He'd watched them eat, watched Reilly walk up the stairs, his intent clear. The guy was in love with his sister; that much was obvious.

A little while later the upstairs lights had gone dark. Tony had stopped thinking about what was happening with his sister and her lover, and gone back to ruminating over his plan.

He was playing several sides against the middle—a dangerous strategy. He was working for the Feds on one side—plea-bargaining for himself by bringing his uncle to them, setting him up to murder Maria and Reilly, and having him caught before he actually did it. Undercover officers would be hidden and in place before Bruno showed up, once Tony gave them the go-ahead.

On another side of the fence, Tony had approached Paul Germano, Bruno's boss. It was a risky move, to say the least. Bruno had been a thorn in Paul's side for a good, long while. There'd been mutterings from time to time that Paul was fed up with Bruno, and that he wanted him out of the picture. Bruno was too unpredictable; he drew too much of the wrong kind of attention.

Tony had known better than to tell Paul about his little arrangement with the Feds, although he had made a bold deal. Tony told Paul he wanted out—he wanted his sister to be able to come home to his mother, he wanted to avenge his father and brother and he wanted his family out of the business for good.

He'd asked for what would have been impossible any other way. He asked Paul to let them out, in exchange for taking down Bruno. Tony was all that was left of that branch of the family, he'd argued, after Bruno was gone. Maria and his mother were all he had left.

Tony said he'd get Bruno out of the picture, permanently, and Paul would forget Tony and his family had ever been part of the organization. They'd make sure Maria was safe from Bruno, no matter what it took.

Amazingly, Paul had agreed. Why not? He had everything to gain, nothing to lose. Nevertheless, if he'd known Tony was simultaneously talking to the Feds, he would have killed him on the spot. Instead, Tony sat, alive, cold, with a crick in his neck and coffee in his lap.

Well, nothing good ever came easy, did it? He knew the end of this wouldn't catch much of a prize for him. He'd be indicted with his uncle—he'd committed crimes that couldn't be washed away. He'd managed not to kill anyone, however, he'd stood by while others were killed, and he'd done some other things he wasn't proud of. His prison term would be reduced because of his help—by how long he didn't know yet.

It didn't matter—all that mattered was settling the score with Bruno, and reuniting his family. If this worked out, he could serve his time peacefully. And since he was being arrested, as well, Bruno would never know his nephew had been behind it.

A movement on the porch across the street caught his eye, interrupting his thoughts. He saw Maria step out into the gray morning light. Seeing her was what he needed to reaffirm that everything he was doing, all he was risking, was worth it.

Bruno wouldn't get to her; Tony would die, first, if he had to. If he died, he planned on taking Bruno with him. Then Maria really would be free.

A few seconds later, Reilly came out on the porch, as well. He walked up behind Maria, slid his hands around her waist and hugged her against him. Tony sighed. He'd checked Reilly out. He was young, younger than him and Maria, but he was a good man. He wasn't Italian, which would give Mama some minor fits, still she'd be so happy to have Maria home, Tony was sure it wouldn't make that big of a difference. If they had any kids, Mama would love them, Irish or whatever.

He smiled, watching his sister lean back into her lover's embrace, and pulled his cell phone out of his pocket, pressing the quick dial.

"Hey. It's me. I need to talk to my uncle."

Bruno hated cell phones and never used them, believing outsiders could listen in too easily. He was probably right to be paranoid. Tony always had to wait and call him at the barber shop, on the regular line. He waited until his uncle's gruff voice asked him what his status was.

"I've got that package you wanted, Tio. I'm holding on to it right now. You want me to mail it?" They always talked in code; mob guys always assumed someone was listening, though in this case, little did Bruno know that his enemy was on the other side of the line.

Bruno was dead silent, and simply asked for directions to the farm. His single command brooked no argument.

"You keep it safe. I may come down and join you for a little vacation after all. You can give it to me then."

"Fair enough. I'll send directions."

Tony hung up, and as soon as he did, he redialed his FBI contact.

10

NATHAN GLANCED OVER at Jennie, who was on the phone with Marge. Jennie looked up at him from under long eyelashes, and just a hint of pink touched her cheeks as she smiled. He knew she was thinking of their night together, and he was, too. If they were together for one hundred years, he would always remember that night.

He went over to the counter and popped a frozen bagel in the toaster. They had to leave, and soon. Preferably before Marge returned home, and discovered he was there. It was best that way, in case anyone came asking.

Jennie hung up, and sighed.

"She'll be home in an hour. She's wrapping up some loose ends, then since she has today off she'll be back to grade."

"What did you tell her?"

"About you? Nothing. We should be gone before she gets here."

"Agreed. Did you tell her that?"

Jennie shook her head. "No, I didn't want

anyone who might come looking to know our movements."

He nodded. They were on the same wavelength.

Eating the toasted bagel in a few bites, he wiped the butter from his hands and turned to her as she reached to put the dish she'd used in the sink.

"You all right?"

"Yes. No. I don't know. I had a plan, yesterday. I knew what I was going to do."

"But now?"

She looked at him, her heart in her eyes. He gathered her close, holding tight.

"We're dealing with this together. I talked with Ian last night, and again this morning."

"You didn't tell me?"

He smiled wickedly. "We had better things going on than talking about Ian."

She smiled, as well, though it faded quickly. "It's not safe to go back there."

"You're right. He and EJ are working out a safe house plan for us, in Bethesda. It's EJ's private property, nothing has been run through federal or public channels. We'll go there, and we'll be safe— if they're looking for you in Virginia, they aren't going to find anything."

"Then what?"

"We'll work that out when we get there. Our first goal is to get your name in the clear, and to get you out of the way of the immediate threat."

"I don't know, Nathan…"

"You have to do this, Jen. Remember I mentioned there was some heat on EJ and Ian, as well? It would help put things to rest for good if you came back and spoke to IA."

"They can't still possibly think—"

"They think you're hiding something, that you ran because you were guilty."

She dropped her head to his shoulder. *"Maddon'.* My life is such a mess. Maybe it would have just been better if—"

He tipped her face up, his eyes blazing down into hers. "Don't even think of saying what you're thinking, lady. Things are a mess, but they're not impossible. Okay?"

She nodded.

"I guess there's only one thing left to be said, then." Nathan knew his timing sucked, but for all he knew, this was the last moment they would have alone together for a while. He needed her to know how he felt. He needed to say the words.

"I love you, Maria. I'll stick by you through all of it, and we'll do what we have to do. I love you and I'm not losing you again. Do you understand?"

He watched tears pool in her eyes and rubbed away one that spilled over, smudging the pad of his thumb over her cheek. There was joy mingled in with all of the other emotions he saw in her expression.

"I love you, too. And, yes, I understand. You and me. Through thick and thin."

"Thick and thin," he repeated like a vow, wrapping his arms around her in a tight embrace. They stayed like that for a few minutes, then he became aware of time passing, and Marge's imminent arrival.

"Ready?"

"As ready as I'll ever be."

As they left, walking down the porch steps to where Nathan had hidden his car the night before, she dared to let herself think that maybe they could work things out—just maybe all wasn't lost yet.

TONY WATCHED as Maria and Reilly left the house, and they didn't look as though they were going out for a walk. They looked as though they were leaving.

This was not good.

Bruno had hopped a flight and would be here within the hour, and the Feds were already on the move. He eyed the electric company truck down the road, and the cable truck that passed, knowing things were already in motion. He'd thought they'd have at least this much time—where could Maria and Reilly be going this early in the morning?

Dammit! Short of holding them hostage, he didn't know what to do. He watched them walk a little ways down the road, and saw Reilly turn into a dirt driveway that looked like a tractor path, pulling back out again in his car. With Maria. Heading in the opposite direction.

"Shit!" He spat out the curse about a million times, just when his cell phone bleeped again— looking down, he closed his eyes and tried to think fast. It was Bruno. He wouldn't be happy if Tony told him he'd lost Maria and Reilly—in fact, Tony probably wouldn't live long past the telling. He ignored the call for a moment, starting the car and driving out from his hiding spot, intending to head back down the road to see where his sister was taking off to now. If he could catch them. If he couldn't...

Then a better option landed before him. A way to get Maria and Nathan back to the house. He watched as a woman—presumably Marge Sawyer—pulled into the driveway and stepped out of her car, completely unaware of his presence.

Marge. They would come back if they believed Marge was in danger—which she was, if he didn't intercede before his uncle and his men arrived at the house.

Tony wrestled with his conscience; he was in a hell of a spot. His idea would put an innocent woman in danger—scare her half to death, certainly. Miss Sawyer would be perfectly safe—if he got to her first.

He cut the engine and got out, crossing the street and reaching for his gun. He apologized under his breath to Miss Sawyer as he ran up the stairs to her home, knocking hard on the door. When she opened it, unsuspecting and with a smile on her face, her eyes held a question—until she saw his gun. He gestured for her to let him in. All of the color drained from her sweet face as she did. He didn't tell her anything more than she wouldn't be hurt. He gave her that much.

It was a desperate plan, but he was a desperate man.

"So TELL ME SOMETHING about your real life—your family," Nathan inquired as they made their way to the interstate. Even though the countryside around them was beautiful, he was only interested in Jennie…*Maria*. From now on, he intended to call her by her real name—there would be no more lies or subterfuge between them.

"I think you know the most important parts."

"I mean something normal. Something good that you remember."

She was quiet for a while, and he knew it must be painful for her to think back. It was part of knowing her, what her life was like before she became Jennie Snow. She sighed heavily before speaking, as if preparing herself.

"Well, okay. You know I was the only girl. I had two younger brothers, Tony and Gino. Gino was the one who…you know."

"Yes. I'm sorry for your loss, and how you lost him." Had anyone ever just told her that? Expressed sympathy for her loss? Nathan wondered. He didn't say anything, encouraging her to continue.

"Well, the three of us were all so different. I was always the bookish one."

He grunted in objection. "That's the last word I would use to describe you, by the way."

"No seriously. I was always reading; I loved school, I made my brothers play school with me when we got home from classes. They hated it. Mama made them go along. It kept them out of her hair, and she knew I would tell on them if they got into anything."

Nathan smiled, imagining a little version of Maria playing schoolteacher.

"Anyway, Tony was the charmer, he had the humor and the smile. At least, when he was young. Girls followed him everywhere. Gino was the softer one, gentle. He loved animals—he'd make my father so angry because he'd never kill so much as an ant. He'd scoop up anything he discovered inside and take it out, find a good spot for it."

"How old was he when he was killed?"

Her smile faltered and she looked back out the window. "Seventeen. Dad was trying to get him to take some small part in the business, and he just didn't want anything to do with it. I think if he'd had the chance, he would have left for good. He was close to Mama, as well, more so than any of us, and it was difficult. There were no easy choices."

Her voice had turned harsh. Thinking of his own boisterous, loving family, he knew he couldn't even imagine what she was describing.

"Anyway, Tony, well, he wanted to go to college. Dad okayed it, if he would study business, become a lawyer, you know, do something that would eventually put him in a stronger position to help the family."

"Tony didn't want that?"

"No. He used to draw in secret. Paint, sometimes, too. He knew our father wouldn't stand for it—he'd think Tony was homosexual or something stupid like that. So, I think Tony just gave up. He gave in. And with Dad gone, he'd have no choice but to work with Bruno."

"Or end up dead. It sounds like Gino might have been milder mannered, but he stood up to your Dad. Tony had a harder time?"

"Probably. He always wanted Dad's acceptance. Middle child syndrome, I guess."

Nathan had no idea what to say and simply reached over to squeeze her hand. He was excused from having to respond when a strange jangling filled the car, and Jennie frowned, reaching into her bag for the disposable cell phone she hadn't even used yet.

"I thought I'd shut this off."

"Oh, I used it this morning, to call Ian. I thought they might be looking for my transmissions. Sorry, I must have forgotten to click it off. Who'd be calling you? Must be a wrong number."

Jennie looked at the number displayed on the screen, and it was familiar. Apprehensively, she answered the call.

"Hello?"

"Hey, sis, long time."

Jennie nearly dropped the phone, grabbing it at the last second with fingers that had turned to ice. She looked quickly behind and around them on the road. There was no one close by. They weren't being followed.

"Tony." She could only whisper one word.

Nathan pulled to the side in a screeching halt within seconds of hearing her utter the name.

"I'm flattered. You recognize my voice after all this time."

"How did you find me? What do you want? How did you get this number?"

"Right to the point, I see. A friend of yours gave it to me."

Jennie thought hard for a second—who could know? And then the answer dawned with a horrible sense of dread.

"Marge."

"Smart as a whip, as always."

"You have her—you leave her alone, Tony. I don't even know her."

"She's fine, Maria. She's sitting here with me and Uncle Bruno having a nice cup of coffee. We'd like you and your friend to come back and join us. She won't get hurt if you just do as you're told."

Everything in Jennie's world sank around her, and it was all she could do to focus on what her brother was saying to her. She couldn't seem to function;

thankfully Nathan reached over, taking hold of her hand. She met his eyes and drew the strength she needed to respond.

"No way."

"Maria. You know what will happen if you don't come back. Like you said, she was…is, an innocent bystander."

"I'll come by myself. You are not getting your hands on Nathan."

"That's really sweet, sis. It must be love. Remember you're not calling the shots, and don't think we're going to make it so easy for lover boy to get his friends and come to your rescue—both of you here, five minutes ago. And don't try anything cute or you know what happens."

He hung up, and she closed her eyes, anger, fear and disgust overwhelming her. "They have Marge, they have Marge…." She rocked back and forth in the seat. Nathan slid over, gripping her by the shoulders, shaking her gently.

"Maria…*Maria.* C'mon. It's okay, tell me what he said."

She took some deep breaths, steadying herself. "Very simple. We go back to the house, or Marge is dead."

"Shit."

"We have no choice, Nathan. We have to go back."

"Okay, then let's go back. With reinforcements."

"There's no time—we're only thirty minutes

away—they'd never get there in time, or they'd blow the whole thing and they'll kill Marge just because."

"You drive. I'll call EJ and Ian. We'll get back-up, stall them and do what we can to get Marge out of there."

"They said they'd kill her if we come with backup."

"Do you think they're going to let her go if we don't? These aren't exactly people who keep their word, sweetheart."

Nathan didn't wait for her response, and shifted over to her side of the seat while she shimmied into his spot. She was white as a sheet. Although her eyes were flat with fear, there was determination there, too.

"We're coming out of this, Maria. I promise. And we'll bring Marge with us."

She just nodded, turned the car around, and headed back toward the house.

"WE'LL TRY GOING IN the back," Nathan whispered, kneeling alongside Maria in the dirt by the shrubs that ran down the side of the house.

"It's too quiet. This isn't good."

Nathan agreed—he would have expected there to be someone at both doors. Marge's car was in the driveway, and there was another car parked by the side of the road across the street, but no one was around except for the electrical crew working down the road.

"I go first," Nathan whispered, and Jennie shook her head firmly.

"If you go at all, we go together."

She was shaking, scared to death about something happening to Nathan or Marge. She wasn't concerned about herself; halfway back to the house, it dawned upon her that she was almost feeling relieved. Soon, one way or the other, this would be over. And even though she might not live to tell about it, she would make sure she lived long enough to spit in her uncle's face before she went.

"Okay. One, two, let's go."

They approached the house, crawling up on the back porch, and peering through a window.

"I don't see anything. This is freakin' weird."

Ignoring Nathan's silent objections, she stood and walked in the door. She doubted she'd be shot on sight—Bruno would want to toy with her first.

"Tony? Marge?"

She walked farther into the kitchen. He hadn't been kidding, she realized, seeing three coffee cups on the table. She slipped her hand around one. Still warm. She turned, finding Nathan directly on her heels.

"We need to get out. It's a trap."

She knew what he was thinking. Bomb. That would be too impersonal for Bruno. He wouldn't kill her long-distance when he had the chance to look in her face and do it up close and personal.

"No, that's not it...."

She peered around the room, and spotted it. A piece of Marge's stationary stuck to the doorjamb with a steak knife. Nice. She grabbed it.

"It's a map. Looks like Marge's handwriting. It's barely legible. She's probably frightened out of her mind." He removed it from the wall, using a towel and dropping the map and the knife into a sandwich bag to protect any prints.

"Where?"

Jennie took the crudely drawn map and studied it. The route signs were clearly marked as was the path to the place.

"I guess we can assume this is where they want us to go."

"Why move? Why take that chance?"

"Too big of a risk of getting caught here. Someone could come by, a friend, someone could call and wonder why Marge's car is in the driveway when she's not answering the phone. It's her home—they'd want to go somewhere more protected, more private," Jennie explained in a soft voice, hoping against hope that Marge was still alive. She'd never forgive herself…

"Let's go."

"Wait…" Jennie paused, staring at the map. "I want to check something out first."

Nathan followed without comment as she went over to the computer on Marge's desk, pulling up an Internet Web site with satellite map images. She found Marge's house on the map.

Flattening the map against the screen, she traced the rough route it offered on the TerraServer, and found it led them to a large parcel of farmland. There was a house, several large barns and some outbuildings.

"I'll bet this is it. The farm may be abandoned by now, these satellite photos aren't recent."

"Amazing what you can find on the Web."

"True—and this is public material. If I were at work, I could get a shot that would almost allow me to look in the windows. And it would be much more up to date."

"Maybe we should call EJ and Ian, have them do that?"

"No, it'll take too much time. This will work—it gives us some escape routes, some different approaches. Maybe we can catch them off guard if we come in this way." She pointed to some dirt roads connected to the farmland and fields, not roads as much as wide paths worn in the dirt.

Nathan paced away from the desk. "Makes sense. We definitely need backup. I'm going to call Ian, and we'll—*agh!*"

Jennie winced as she tried to catch Nathan when his knees gave; she couldn't hold his weight altogether. At least she was able to break his fall a little, and keep him from hitting the edge of the desk on the way down.

The heavy bookend with which she'd clocked him had fallen to the side. She checked his pulse, easing a hand over his forehead to push his hair back—

she'd given him a good lump. Guilt flooded her as she checked his pupils, and then she let it go—he was out cold, maybe slightly concussed, still he'd be better off that way than dead.

She wasn't about to have Bruno and Tony take one more person she loved away from her. As much as Nathan thought they could face this together and win, she knew differently. She wasn't letting him die. Maybe he'd hate her, maybe he'd mourn her, though at least he'd be alive to do it.

Bending down, she didn't bother biting back tears as she kissed him gently on the forehead, whispering her love for him before leaving him while she still had the strength and the will to do it. Finding Marge's keys still on the stand by the door where she left them, Maria headed out to face her fate without so much as a single glance backward.

11

NATHAN OPENED HIS EYES, first noticing the rough weave of green carpet pressed up against his face, and then the splitting pain that made his stomach retch as he tried to move.

"Jen...dammit, ow..."

He sat up, slowly, his head still spinning like crazy. What had hit him? Was Jen okay? Obviously they hadn't been alone in the house as they'd thought. Fear for what had happened to her when he was conked out drove him to his feet despite the pain and nausea.

Calling out, he heard no response. No sign of a struggle, no evidence that she'd been taken or hurt.

He kicked something as he walked back to the desk, and he looked down, finding the heavy bookend lying on the floor and putting two-and-two together much faster than he was comfortable with. No one had taken Jen—she'd taken him out. He didn't have to ask why; she was intent on facing down her family alone. And probably getting herself and Marge killed. Bruno and Tony Castone would never allow either woman to get out of that barn alive.

He took out his cell phone at the same time he clicked on the computer screen, clearing the screen saver and breathing a sigh of relief that she hadn't stopped to close down the image. He could remember the path on the rough map they'd traced, and he spoke urgently as he stared at the screen, committing it to memory as he checked his watch to see how much of a lead she had on him.

"Ian, get EJ on the line—we have a big problem."

"WHAT'S TAKING SO LONG?"

Tony stood by the doorway of the barn they waited in, his nerves on a razor's edge as they waited for his sister's arrival. The woman from the house, Marge, sat tied and shivering on the floor, and Tony was worried—she wasn't dressed warmly and was at risk for hypothermia. She'd be at risk of a lot worse, if his uncle got much more impatient. Guilt chipped away at Tony's certainty that his plan would still work. How would he live with it if something happened to this poor woman?

So many things had gone wrong; he hadn't counted on his uncle getting spooked by the mailman's arrival at the door, and the resulting insistence that they move. Too public, he said. Too messy.

Tony prayed that the federal agents monitoring the scene had been able to follow. He had no doubt Maria would appear—she would never let her friend die in her place. Bruno knew it, too.

"This is a bust, we need to get out of here. Lose the broad and let's go."

Tony's anxiety spiked. Marge looked up at them, at him, from the floor with terrified eyes, and he wished he could send her some kind of signal that everything would be all right. To keep them all alive, Bruno couldn't suspect that Tony was any less than one hundred percent committed to the cause.

"Be patient. She'll be here. This would have been over and done with if you hadn't moved the location."

"It was stupid to meet at that house—too many people around, too many interruptions. You should have known better."

Something like sleet started falling, making the landscape even more bleak. Two other men were located at the other corners of the barn. He'd better spot his sister first. He had to keep as much control of this situation as he could, now that it had become so unpredictable. Federal agents or not, he'd do what he had to to keep his sister and Marge Sawyer alive, though at the moment he was facing three-to-one odds.

Not great, but doable.

"We're going," his uncle declared, motioning to one of his flunkies to deal with Marge, and Tony slid his hand inside his jacket, reaching for his own gun when he heard a voice—Maria's voice. Shocked, they all turned to see her standing on the far side of the barn—how the hell did she do that?

"Tony." Her eyes were cold as they met his, and then pinned a hard stare on Bruno. "Uncle B." She addressed Bruno belligerently with the nickname he hated, a sign of complete disrespect, and he saw his uncle's shoulders stiffen. Tony almost smiled; his sister had balls.

She looked as if she'd been through hell, but she didn't look afraid. The forty-five, semiautomatic she had pointed in their direction probably had something to do with that. He'd forgotten for a moment, she was a cop. She had skills.

He wondered if she had backup—where was Reilly? He thought he'd caught some movement out of the corner of his eye, outside the barn, still he didn't dare lose track of the drama playing out in front of him. Bruno stepped forward, facing his niece without seeming to care about the cannon she was aiming in his direction. You didn't attain Bruno's position in the organization if you were scared of standing behind a gun. Or in front of one.

"Maria. You came."

"You thought I wouldn't?" Maria cast him a withering look, as if her uncle was the least of her concerns, and then swung her gaze in Marge's direction. "Let her go. You have what you came here for."

"Maybe later. Maybe not."

Tony saw it again—there was definitely someone else out there. Even if it was only Reilly, their numbers were more even now. Setting Bruno up with the Feds may have fallen through. Even so, as long as they all got out of the barn alive, he could deal.

"You're one hard cookie to find, sis. I don't care for the new hair color, either. Makes you look harsh."

"How'd you find me Tony?"

"You're not as invisible as you think you are. Though it was a smart move, hiding out in the one place no one would ever look for you, right smack in the middle of the federal government."

"Thanks. I live for your approval."

Something flickered in her eyes, and he noticed her distraction, even though it lasted only for a second. She'd seen it, too. Noticed the movement outside the barn.

"You always were a smart-ass."

"While we're here, let me ask you, Tony, how could you do it? How could you turn your back on what this…piece of garbage…did to our family?"

Bruno cut in. "Because he knows how to stay alive, which is more than I can say for you. Did you think you'd testify against me and get off clean? Did you think I'd let you walk away?"

"I did walk away."

"You didn't get far." Bruno took out his own gun, and the men on either side of the barn did likewise. He smiled, a sickening, greasy smile. "You won't walk away this time. But before I watch you die— and it won't be fast, by the way—I want to know where your partner is."

"I don't know what you mean."

Tony's heart tightened in his chest as he saw Bruno motion to one of his goons to get Marge— obviously he planned to use Marge to compel Maria to tell him whatever he needed to know.

Tony got to her first. He helped her to her feet, and lugged her limp, trembling body up against him. He saw Maria's eyes narrow as she looked over at him. In case he was giving too much away, he drew out his own gun, shoving it up underneath Marge's chin and steeling himself to ignore her whimper of fear— there was no way he could reveal he was trying to save her life, not take it.

"Talk, Maria, or this will get messy. Where's your cop lover?"

That hit a nerve; she visibly paled.

"He's not with me."

"No kidding. Took off when things got too hot?"

"I hit him. I left him behind."

"What kind of man lets a woman get the best of him? What's the world coming to?" Bruno asked the question as if he were having a conversation with friends over coffee, then his eyes turned taunting and deadly. "We used him to find you, you know."

She shook her head. Bruno just laughed.

"My sweet little Maria, we put a tracking device on him, and knew where he was every minute of the day, and the night. Knew *everything* he was doing."

"You sonofabitch."

"So where is he, sweetheart?"

"He's right here," Nathan's voice came from behind them, and they all turned to find him standing against the side of the barn, staring at them as if he didn't have four loaded guns facing him.

The kid had more than enough cool, Tony would give him that. Seeing as he also appeared to be unarmed, he was also in a hell of a lot of trouble. They both were.

JENNIE DIDN'T KNOW HOW to react when Nathan showed up on the other side of the barn. Apparently she hadn't hit him hard enough. And she had his gun, so he was unarmed.

"Nathan." She spoke his name without really meaning to, and he turned cool eyes in her direction, arching one eyebrow with a questioning look. He probably wasn't too pleased she'd taken off without him.

"Maria."

"You weren't supposed to come."

"You know I'll always find you. I couldn't let you face these...animals...alone."

It still sounded strange to be called by her real name out loud—she hadn't heard it in so long.

"How romantic," Bruno interrupted, his tone laced with sarcasm. "Now I think everyone is here. We can get back down to business." He motioned to Nathan to stand next to Jennie.

Nathan did so, slowly, laconically. He even slanted a smile at her uncle, which made her shoot him a warning look. Although Bruno's business was with her, he'd just as soon shoot Nathan as look at him, if provoked.

"So what now?" Tony asked, still grasping onto Marge.

Jennie didn't want to plead with her brother, though what choice did she have? Family connections clearly didn't matter much to him, still she had to find some way to reach him.

"Tony, please, let her go. You have us. She's not involved."

"She is now," Bruno disagreed. "She's a witness. It's your fault, you know—she dies, it's because of you. Him, too." He glanced at Nathan and Jennie's heart froze, if for no other reason than her uncle was right. This was all her fault. She should have left town sooner, and she never should have let Nathan back into her life. If he died, it was because she'd been weak.

"You won't breathe a word, will you, Marge?"

Trembling, Marge shook her head.

"She doesn't know my real name, she doesn't know you. She's seen you. Still she has no idea who we are. Let her go. She knows you can find her again if she tries anything, right, Marge?"

Again, Marge nodded so hard she shook in Tony's grasp. Her uncle wasn't buying it. This was going to get ugly. She'd only fired a gun in training—she'd never killed anyone, never had to fire a gun for real. She better be able to do it now.

"You know," Bruno spoke slowly, his gun now focused on Nathan, "I think having two cops at our disposal could be a little bonus—maybe there are some things you could tell us before we kill you."

Jennie managed an incredulous snort, "Yeah, right. Like that's great incentive."

"Drop your gun."

"I don't think so, Uncle B."

"Then he gets one in the stomach—very painful. One…" He cocked the hammer back, and Jennie was frantic, trying to figure out if she could shoot him before he shot Nathan, and if any of them would stand a chance if Bruno's men opened fire in response.

"Two…"

She tried to steady her hand, but before he could finalize his count, she looked at Nathan in apology, and dropped the gun, kicking it out in front of them.

"I thought you'd see things my way."

"You're scum," Jennie spat out the words.

"And you are a traitor to your family."

Everyone in the barn jumped a little when she laughed, loud and unexpectedly, and without humor.

"Me? A traitor to my family? You killed your own brother, and your nephew—who was completely innocent. Gino had never hurt a fly."

"Shows how much you know, little girl. Do you think that was just some random grab for power?"

"Yes."

Bruno glared at her. "Your youngest brother had been wearing a wire for some time—looks like you and he have a lot in common. He'd been feeding them information about all of us, and apparently had turned over enough on your father that they'd forced him to go belly up, as well. Believe me, your father would rather have been taken out of this life than have gone to prison on the testimony of his traitorous son."

"I don't believe you," Jennie whispered, amazed that her brother Gino had been involved in such activity. Was that what he'd been trying to call her about the week before he was killed? How could she have been involved in Federal Law Enforcement for so many years, and not have known this? Bruno must be lying.

"I don't care what you believe. You, your brother and even your father—weak, traitors, the lot of you. Only Tony turned out right. I wasn't sure of him, but he's proved himself."

Jennie slid a derisive look toward her brother, who had remained silent during the exchange as he continued holding Marge hostage.

"Yeah, he's really turned out well. What's it feel like, Tony, selling your soul to hell? How's Mama, by the way? Does she know who you really are? That you work for the man who took Daddy and Gino from her?"

"Mama understands things are…complicated."

"Yeah, right. Complicated. You're a killer, and you're his stooge. What's complicated about that?"

She saw a flicker of something in Tony's face, and it made her pause—guilt? She couldn't be sure. It disappeared so swiftly she wasn't certain if she had actually seen anything. Maybe she could reach him, maybe, if she pushed hard enough.

"How do you live with yourself, Tony? Standing by the man who killed Gino, standing there and watching him kill again. I remember when we were kids, Tony. You used to stand up for Gino, and for me. You protected us, even when we didn't need it. You were good—you *are* good—you just have to look down deep—"

"Enough!" Bruno ordered. She knew her moment to reach her brother had passed. She saw her uncle's face screw into a nasty snarl. "He's not listening to you, *puttana.* He listens only to me. Your precious brother would have killed you himself if I'd let him—he doesn't take a piss unless I say so, so save your breath."

"Say what you want, Bruno. You can't hurt me anymore."

When Bruno took aim at Nathan, she felt her muscles tense as she readied to push Nathan out of the way.

"I can hurt you, Maria, and I'm going to prove it by putting a bullet through your lover first."

Jennie pushed off from her stance, slamming hard into Nathan, who also seemed to have jumped toward her, following the same impulse to protect her, as well. They knocked each other to the ground as bullets zipped over their heads. Guns fired, and everyone flew for cover.

Jennie felt Nathan flattening her to the dirty barn floor. She tried to get grit out of her eyes to see what was happening.

Marge, and one of Bruno's men, were on the floor, and there was a blaring noise outside the barn, tires ripping through the mud, and the screeching sounds of sirens. Backup—Nathan must have not come in alone. Although the gunfire quieted, she stayed down.

Peering around the barn, she heard car doors and someone shouting from outside. She couldn't hear what they were saying. Then she saw Bruno standing over Nathan, who'd leaped up from his hiding spot, lunging for the gun she'd thrown to the ground, and hadn't quite made it.

Bruno looked like a madman; it was clear he wasn't going down without trying to take someone with him. As her heart caught in her throat, Jennie emerged from her cover, to draw his fire to her if she could. Bruno was hit from behind, his back arching forward as a large exit wound made itself apparent on the front of his jacket.

She looked up, expecting to see Federal marshals or FBI as the shooter who'd saved Nathan. Instead she saw her brother, Tony, the gun he'd pointed at their uncle still in his steady grip.

As agents rushed into the barn, Jennie stared at her

brother and Nathan, who stared back just as incred-
ulously. Tony knelt by Marge's body, put his hand
to her neck and smiled. He gave a thumbs-up to
Jennie—right before agents surrounded him and told
him to back away.

Jennie rushed to Nathan's side, falling to the floor
beside him.

"Oh, my God, are you hurt, did he shoot you...are
you okay?" The questions came out rapid-fire as she
patted him down everywhere, desperate to make sure
he was okay. Nathan grabbed her hands and looked
into her face.

"I'm fine—Tony helped me out there."

"I saw," she responded in hushed tones, looking over
to where agents had handcuffed her brother to a rail at
the side of the barn, and EMTs were attending to
Marge. Poor Marge. She'd be traumatized, for sure. At
least she'd walk away, and that's what mattered most.
Would they still be friends, or would Marge never want
to see her face again? Not that she could blame her.

Her gaze swung back to her brother. "I can't believe
it. I can't believe I actually got through to him."

Nathan stood, dusting himself off, taking in
Bruno's dead body, studying the man who'd been
about to shoot him and the woman he loved.

"I think Tony probably did hear you—I'm sure
you reached him on some level. There's more to it
than that, I suspect."

"What do you mean?"

Nathan looked in Tony's direction, the look he sent the other man confirming that he knew what had passed between them, and he wasn't going to forget it.

"After I came to—my head still hurts, by the way…"

Jennie felt a sharp twinge of guilt. "I know, I'm so sorry. I was trying to save your life."

"By cracking my skull?"

"What did you mean about Tony?" She decided to sidestep the knocking-out discussion for as long as she could.

"I called Ian and EJ, let them know you'd ditched me, and they dug in fast and found out that Feds were already on the premises, part of a separate operation centered on taking Bruno Castone down."

"How could we have not known about that?"

"You know the government—half the time the left side doesn't know what the right side is doing, and all that. In this case, with even a hint of suspicion about a leak from our department, they wouldn't exactly have been in a sharing mood."

"Incredible."

"Anyway, this other operation was kicked into play by your brother Tony. Apparently he'd been looking for you for a long while, and used Bruno's resources to help him do it—under the cover of wanting to help his uncle find you. He went to the FBI, told them about the plan and the rest is history."

Jennie was shocked. Her brother had been working against her uncle all this time? She cast another glance toward him, their eyes meeting. This was all so overwhelming, and she felt a little light-headed.

"Hey, c'mere. You look like you're going to fall over."

"I'm fine, it's just a lot to process. And it's been a hell of a day."

"True enough. Anyway, he'd found you on his own before they did, and he used it as a way to get rid of Bruno for good. He dragged Bruno along for a while, pretending not to know where you were."

"So the mole story was a part of it?"

"Yeah. They leaked that in order to make Bruno and any cronies he has in the program think Tony was actually following through. They didn't expect you to run, though, and they'd tagged my cell phone, which is the only way they found us here. Tony's plan almost went south big-time today. Nevertheless, he accomplished his goal, more or less." Again, they both looked at Bruno's body, and Jennie shivered. Was her nightmare really over? It didn't seem possible. There was always someone new to take a boss's place.

"So you knew all this when you came in, that Tony was working with the Feds?"

"Yeah, pretty much. I was on the phone with EJ and Ian, and they filled me in. Then I hooked up with some of the local guys and they let me go in ahead. I figured that helped our numbers."

"Marge…"

"An unforeseen element of the plan not going exactly as it was supposed to. Bruno was en route to Marge's as we left—she would have been there when he arrived. Tony had to think fast, protect her and get us back here for the sting to go down."

"Then they changed locations...."

"Another twist."

Jennie looked up at Nathan. "I need to see my brother."

"Take your time, I'll get Ian and EJ on the line, and help clean up here." He started to turn away, then stopped. "And Jen, let Tony know what he did...well, let him know I'll make sure it counts. Big-time."

Jennie nodded, feeling a little like she was in the twilight zone as she walked over to where her brother, whom she hadn't seen in over a decade, stood handcuffed to a rail. Cops, crime scene investigators, ambulances, people were swarming everywhere, yet she was focused only on Tony. She brushed off an EMT trying to waylay her with questions, continuing to move forward.

"Let him out of the cuffs," she instructed one of the rookies standing guard, her voice as soft as could be. The guy started to object, red spreading from his neck to his ears, and she gave him a look that bore no objection.

"You free him now, or I'll make sure this is the last major operation you ever take part in."

She didn't have that power, of course, however the

rookie wouldn't know that. As it turned out, an agent she'd worked with once or twice was also on the scene and overheard her—and summarily gave the rookie permission to do as he was told.

She smiled as he backed off, thanking him. She also couldn't believe her brother, standing there, handsome as she remembered—more so—was laughing.

"You want me to leave you there?"

"Oh, God, how I've missed you, Maria."

She had no words. All she could do was stand before her brother, taking in the man he had become. He was taller than she was, and he'd filled out. He was handsome, of course, his brown eyes just like hers, dancing with mischief as she looked him over, and then filling with love and concern.

"Ah, Maria. It's all going to be okay. I promise."

That was what she used to tell her brothers when they were little and she had comforted them on so many occasions. It was what he'd said to her after their father and brother were gone, but she'd been so out of it, so ravaged with grief and rage, she hadn't really listened to what he was telling her then.

She was listening now. Could there ever be anything like "normal" after what they'd been through? There were too many things racing around her brain, too many questions, too many emotions to handle. She couldn't find words. Instead, she just fell into her brother's strong arms and cried and cried and cried.

12

"I TAKE IT MARIA is not going to be in this morning? How's she holding up?" Ian glanced around the conference table, noting the empty chair. It had been a week since the takedown, and things were getting more or less back to normal. Which meant he needed his team together; there was work to do.

Nathan nodded. Everyone knew that Maria—they were all getting used to using her real name now—wasn't in because she was spending the day with her brother before he started his prison term.

It was a heart-wrenching situation; though Tony's sentence had been reduced considerably, and with good behavior he'd be paroled in a few years, it was still difficult. Maria felt as though she'd regained her family only to be losing her brother again, and it wasn't easy.

"She's holding up—mostly for him. She's amazingly strong."

"Stronger than you, from what I saw of the knot on the back of your head," Sarah taunted from across the table, lightening the mood.

EJ grinned, piping in, "We exerted what pull we

could. He'll spend most of his time in minimum security, and within driving distance. Believe me, he'll be okay. Bruno is gone, and apparently one of Tony's moves was to right things with the bigger bosses before he set this plan in motion. So it really is over for the Castones. They're safe now."

Nathan nodded, still amazed at how much had happened in just a few days. "Tony's already a good man. A hero. I hate it that he has to do any time, and it's ripping Maria apart. He just had an impossible situation. Hell, he saved my life, her life—he brought down Bruno. And he's going to freakin' jail?"

Nathan was getting worked up, but Ian cut him some slack. The past few weeks would have been tough on the most seasoned cop, and Nathan had handled it all like a pro. He was entitled.

"It was part of his original deal. He was still involved in some nasty business with his uncle, even if all he did was stand at the sidelines. If he's the kind of man I think he is, Nate, he wouldn't feel right getting off scot-free. He'll be okay," Ian reassured, continuing, "Okay, let's get back to work here. Reports?"

While the others settled in, Nathan remained edgy and worried about Maria. He wished he could be with her, even though he knew she wanted to spend time with her brother alone. He respected that. Since he had no work on his desk, no new assignments, he had nothing to report, and so just listened to what was being said.

As the meeting ended, he stood up, thinking he would just go home and wait for Maria. They'd more or less taken to staying at his place now, ever since they'd returned. Everything had been in such turmoil they hadn't really talked more about their relationship, where things were going. It was clear she loved him, too, though what did that mean? What next?

"Nate, I want you and Maria—man, it still feels weird calling her that—in my office first thing tomorrow. Okay?"

Hmm. That didn't sound good. No work on his desk and a command to show up in the boss's office. Great. He just acknowledged the request, and walked back out to his desk, gathering up his things.

Sarah approached, watching him silently for a moment. His coat over his arm, he looked at her, shrugging.

"What?"

"You okay?"

"Yeah, I'm good."

"You look like shit."

"You're just trying to hide your strong attraction to me, aren't you?"

She laughed, and he felt things loosen up inside a little. At least some things were still reliable, like Sarah harassing him. He realized he would have missed it if he'd left.

"You two are going to work out fine, Nathan. Just give it a little time."

"Thanks, Sarah." On total impulse, he brushed a kiss across her cheek. She drew back, looking around them, and then smacking him soundly on the arm.

"Do that again and I'll take you out, Junior Mint."

"Yeah, you want me and you know it, Lady Amazon."

Their laughter filled the office as he left, feeling a little better. Looking at his watch, he knew it was about the time that Maria would be parting ways with Tony, and he wanted to make sure he was there for her when she arrived home. As he planned to be for many years to come.

"DO ME A FAVOR, WOULD YOU?"

Tony sat in the passenger seat where they were parked outside of the federal building. When he left the car, he'd be walking up the steps to surrender the next three years of his life, minimum. *It just wasn't fair!* Jennie thought furiously, biting back tears that just seemed to keep coming no matter how many she gave way to. She squeezed her brother's hand.

"Anything."

"Go see Gino when you go home—let him know we did it. We made things right."

She absolutely planned to visit their brother's gravesite now that she was free and safe to do so. She couldn't believe that she could go home, that she could use her real name, get on with her life. All because of Tony.

"*You* made things right. I'll tell him that. I wish you could come with me."

"Soon enough. It's only a few years. A small price to pay for a clean conscience. A new start."

"You don't deserve this. You were trapped as much as I was all those years, worse, even. What could you do but go along? He would have killed you."

Her outrage made him smile. He was such a good man, her brother. She ran a hand over the curly brown hair that was just the same as he'd had as a boy. He smiled, grabbing her hand and kissing it.

"No more tears, Maria. Things will be fine. I'm okay with this. I'm better than okay, knowing you're free to come back to us now. The time will pass quickly."

"I hope so."

His eyes danced with humor. "So you and Nathan, huh? Will I have nieces and nephews by the time I'm released?"

She threw her hands up, laughing. "You sound like Mama!"

She'd only talked to her mother on the phone. It had been wonderful, tearful, and she was going home soon to visit. Her mother was stronger about Tony going to prison; she was proud of him for doing the right thing. Maria—it was another freedom to be able to reclaim her real name, even for herself—could only imagine the care packages of cookies and such that Tony would be receiving. Somehow, it made everything a little better.

"Sorry, *carina,* you are getting up there, no time to waste."

She laughed, experiencing pure joy at being able to be teased by her younger brother.

"Well, we'll just see about that."

He gazed out the window at the courthouse steps. "He's a good man. He loves you. I'm glad you found him."

"Me, too. And neither of us will ever forget what you've done, what you've sacrificed."

He drew her over into a hard hug.

"You'll visit? Write?"

"Constantly."

He reached for the door, and it was all she could do not to pull him back. She'd wanted to go inside with him, but he refused. He didn't want her to see him being taken away. Words choked in her throat.

"Love you, Tony."

"Love you, too, sis. See you soon."

She wasn't able to drive home until her vision cleared. She went home—to Nathan's—and saw the lights warming his windows. He'd be there, waiting, and she needed his arms so badly tonight.

When she stepped into the apartment, something smelled delicious. She was starving, too tightly strung to eat much even though she'd taken Tony out to a good lunch.

"Nathan?"

"In here, babe."

She wandered into the kitchen, and felt her worry melt away, replaced by a flow of love and lust. Nathan was dressed in worn jeans and an old T-shirt that claimed, FBI: Full-Blooded Irish on the back in faded green letters. He looked good enough to eat, pulling a spoon out of the pot he was tending and setting it on the counter before he crossed the kitchen and wrapped her in his arms, which was just what she needed.

"You okay?"

"Yeah. It's going to be okay."

"I wish it didn't have to happen. He seemed like a stand-up guy. I'd like to get to know him better."

"He liked you, too. He's already counting on nieces and nephews." She blushed, realizing what she'd actually said and looked past his shoulder, toward the stove, changing the subject. "What's that? I could smell it down the hall, and it has my mouth watering."

He peered into her face with a mischievous smile, "It's lamb stew—my aunt's recipe from Ireland. As for making your mouth water, I thought I did that?"

"I have to admit, seeing you in the kitchen in those jeans doesn't hurt any."

"You like that, do you, a man in the kitchen?"

She returned his mischievous smile, glancing down at the floor. "And barefoot, at that."

He laughed, lowering his lips to hers and kissing her so thoroughly and with such mounting desire she wondered why food had ever been a priority. She would never need food again if he would just keep kissing her like this, she thought, sighing with satisfaction as his tongue explored her mouth, and his hands started a very nice journey over her skin.

He felt wonderful. Suddenly everything that felt heavy and horrible in life lifted. She sighed again as Nathan pushed her gently back against the wall, intent on doing more than touching, apparently.

"What do you think about that, Nate?" she asked between kisses.

"About what?"

"About Tony wanting some nieces and nephews?"

At first she worried her timing may have been less than perfect, and she didn't want to kill the mood, yet when she saw how dark his eyes were, how emotion had softened his face and how desire had seemed to multiply tenfold, she realized her timing maybe wasn't that bad at all.

"I think you can stop taking your birth control any time you darned well please."

She laughed joyfully as he buried his face in her neck, creating the most wonderful sensations.

"I think my poor mother has had enough to deal with—she hasn't even seen me for more than ten years. I probably owe her a legitimate grandchild in good time, at the very least."

Nathan grinned wickedly. "Maria Castone, are you asking me to marry you?"

Feeling cheeky, joyful and so full of happiness she

could hardly stand it, she laughed. "Maybe. Would that bother you?"

He fell to his knees at her feet, kissing her hand and looking up at her with such love, lust and devotion she thought she was going to cry—again.

"Well, now I may have cooked dinner. And I may have been waiting for you to come home dressed sexy and barefoot…"

She grinned as he affected the Irish brogue that he'd told her his grandfather taught him, and he was right, it did make her heart flutter.

"…but I'll be the one who'll be doing the askin', my love." He smiled more seriously.

"Will you be my wife, Maria? You can say when, I don't care, but I don't want you out of my life for one single day, ever again. You're the love of my heart."

"And you're mine. I love you, Nathan. Of course I'll marry you."

They stared at each other, the future in their eyes. The sizzling noise of the stew boiling over broke the spell and had him jumping up from the floor to save their dinner, turning off the heat.

Crisis averted, he turned to her again where she stood smiling. What a beauty. The fact that they could be together for the rest of their lives, that they would have a family together, moved him as nothing else ever had.

"I forgot to mention, Ian wants us both in the office tomorrow morning."

"Did he say why?" Maria decided that dinner could wait. Shrugging off her jacket, she stretched, making sure she arched her back just right so that the blouse she wore accentuated her breasts for his view. She was going to make her new fiancé's mouth water.

Indeed, when she lowered her arms, his eyes were glued, though his voice was normal.

"He didn't. I didn't find any new assignments on my desk today, though. I'm a little worried we may have both pushed the envelope a little too far this time."

She unbuttoned the blouse slowly, slipping it down her arms and tossing it to the chair. "I'm sure if he wanted to fire you, he would have done it. It's probably just lecture time."

The flirty pout she affected had his cock rocketing in his jeans, but he was enjoying the show, and sat back to watch.

"Yeah, you're probably right. Aren't you a little worried, though?"

She shimmied out of the skirt and slipped her heels off. Standing before him in just a slip of silk panties and her bra, she ran her hands through her hair, which had been returned to its normal, rich brown.

"Not really. No, I'm not worried at all at the moment."

"Hungry?"

"As good as that stew smells, I think I'd rather wait on dinner."

She released the clasp on her bra, and Nathan was across the kitchen in a flash, pulling her nearly naked form up against him. There was only so much a guy could take.

"I can't argue with your priorities, babe."

Epilogue

"MAMA, I CAN'T EAT all this. I won't be able to move." Maria sat back, shoving the plate away before her mother heaped more food on it. The woman was trying to make up for every meal she'd missed over ten years, but between having two families cooking for them all the time, Maria was going to be the plumpest cop in the unit. She had to start exercising more just to balance it all out.

"You work long hours—you need fuel."

Nathan winked at her from the other side of the small kitchen table loaded down with food. His metabolism seemed to be dealing far too well with the onslaught of family parties and dinners that had been nearly constant in the week since they'd moved to Boston to head up the new HotWires Unit. That had been the reason Ian wanted to talk to them that morning.

"The hours will level out later. Getting the new team in place, that's taking some time."

Maria looked at Nathan, her tone back to business. "Has Nolan officially accepted the position?"

"I think he will. He'll be perfect. I think Ian had his eye on him. I grabbed him first."

"Good move. So we need one more."

"We have a big fat stack of files to go through tomorrow, and we should be able to start interviews next week. Then we just have to do one more set with Ian or EJ, and we should be up and running."

"It's a superior man, Maria, who can work with a woman and not feel threatened." Her mother winked at her from behind Nathan's chair. The two had taken to each other immediately. Probably because Nathan never turned down seconds and he had already mentioned that if they ever had a boy, he wanted to name him after Gino.

"Don't do that, Mama. His head is big enough."

Her cheeks heated as Nathan sent her a secret, naughty look that hooked onto the sexual innuendo in her innocent words. She laughed, shaking her head. She was discovering things about him that she loved more and more every day—including his sense of humor.

"I wish you'd still wait and have a big wedding. You're my only daughter, you should have it all."

She smiled at Nathan, and reached up to hug her mom, something she couldn't quite stop doing.

"I have it all, Mama. We don't want a big fuss. And this way we can be married faster. I just wish Tony could be there. I would have loved for him to give me away. EJ offered to do it and that's special, too. I can't wait for you to meet them all."

Though her mother was sad, she understood that her second oldest was doing what he had to, and had made it possible for them all to be together. They all knew it, and couldn't wait for the day Tony returned.

"He's fine, Mama. Nathan and I talked to him just yesterday. He's taking some art classes."

"I know. I know. He said he would bring you back, and he did. And we'll all be together again, soon enough. And I'm looking forward to meeting your friends. You tell them no hotels—I have so many empty rooms upstairs."

Maria marveled at her mother's strength, and laughed.

"I'll make sure they know."

Her mother started clearing the table and she and Nathan rose to help as she went into the kitchen, saying something about kids being in too much hurry these days.

Nathan laughed. "She's great. We could have a big wedding, if you want to change your mind. We can afford it—the raises that came with taking on the new job make it possible."

"No, I mean it. I don't want to wait. And with work being what it is, it's going to be difficult enough to find time for a honeymoon."

He set his dishes down and looped an arm around her, not quite able to believe his luck. He had Maria, they were getting married in a week and they'd been reassigned by Ian back to Boston to work on forming a local HotWires team. Kissing his wife-to-be, he pulled back, looking into her face.

"Life is good."

As she leaned in for another, deeper kiss, she knew it was going to get even better.

* * * * *

"OH, NO!"

The reaction slipped out before Emma Valentine could stop it, for there stood the very man she most wanted to avoid seeing again.

He didn't look any happier to see her.

"Well, come on, get on board," he said gruffly. "I won't bite." One eyebrow rose. "Though I might nibble a little," he added, mostly to amuse himself.

But she wasn't paying any attention to what he was saying. She was staring at him, taking in the royal blue uniform he was wearing, with gold braid and glistening badges decorating the sleeves, epaulettes and an upright collar. Ribbons and medals covered the breast of the short, fitted jacket. A gold-encrusted sabre hung at his side. And suddenly it was clear to her who this man really was.

She gulped wordlessly. Reaching out, he took her elbow and pulled her aboard. The doors slid closed. And finally she found her tongue.

"You...you're the prince."

He nodded, barely glancing at her. "Yes. Of course."

She raised a hand and covered her mouth for a moment. "I should have known."

"Of course you should have. I don't know why you didn't." He punched the ground-floor button to get the elevator moving again, then turned to look down at her. "A relatively bright five-year-old child would have tumbled to the truth right away."

Her shock faded as her indignation at his tone asserted itself. He might be the prince, but he was still just as annoying as he had been earlier that day.

"A relatively bright five-year-old child without a bump on the head from a badly thrown water polo ball, maybe," she said defensively. She wasn't feeling woozy any longer and she wasn't about to let him bully her, no matter how royal he was. "I was unconscious half the time."

"And just clueless the other half, I guess," he said, looking bemused.

The arrogance of the man was really galling.

"I suppose you think your 'royalness' is so obvious it sort of shimmers around you for all to see?" she challenged. "Or better yet, oozes from your pores like…like sweat on a hot day?"

"Something like that," he acknowledged calmly. "Most people tumble to it pretty quickly. In fact, it's hard to hide even when I want to avoid dealing with it."

"Poor baby," she said, still resenting his manner. "I guess that works better with injured people who are half asleep." Looking at him, she felt a strange emotion she couldn't identify. It was as though she wanted to prove something to him, but she wasn't sure what. "And anyway, you know you did your best to fool me," she added.

His brows knit together as though he really didn't know what she was talking about. "I didn't do a thing."

"You told me your name was Monty."

"It is." He shrugged. "I have a lot of names. Some of them are too rude to be spoken to my face, I'm sure." He glanced at her sideways, his hand on the hilt of his sabre. "Perhaps you're contemplating one of those right now."

You bet I am.

That was what she would like to say. But it suddenly occurred to her that she was supposed to be working for this man. If she wanted to keep the job of coronation chef, maybe she'd better keep her opinions to herself. So she clamped her mouth shut, took a deep breath and looked away, trying hard to calm down.

The elevator ground to a halt and the doors slid open laboriously. She moved to step forward, hoping to make her escape, but his hand shot out again and caught her elbow.

"Wait a minute. *You're* a woman," he said, as though that thought had just presented itself to him.

"That's a rare ability for insight you have there, Your Highness," she snapped before she could stop herself. And then she winced. She was going to have to do better than that if she was going to keep this relationship on an even keel.

But he was ignoring her dig. Nodding, he stared at her with a speculative gleam in his golden eyes. "I've been looking for a woman, but you'll do."

She blanched, stiffening. "I'll do for what?"

He made a head gesture in a direction she knew was opposite of where she was going and his grip tightened on her elbow.

"Come with me," he said abruptly, making it an order.

She dug in her heels, thinking fast. She didn't much like orders. "Wait! I can't. I have to get to the kitchen."

"Not yet. I need you."

"You what?" Her breathless gasp of surprise was soft, but she knew he'd heard it.

"I need you," he said firmly. "Oh, don't look so shocked. I'm not planning to throw you into the hay and have my way with you. I need you for something a bit more mundane than that."

She felt color rushing into her cheeks and she silently begged it to stop. Here she was, formless and stodgy in her chef's whites. No makeup, no stiletto heels. Hardly the picture of the femmes fatales he was undoubtedly used to. The likelihood that he would have any carnal interest in her was remote at best. To have him think she was hysterically defending her virtue was humiliating.

"Well, what if I don't want to go with you?" she said in hopes of deflecting his attention from her blush.

"Too bad."

"What?"

Amusement sparkled in his eyes. He was certainly enjoying this. And that only made her more determined to resist him.

"I'm the prince, remember? And we're in the castle. My orders take precedence. It's that old pesky divine rights thing."

Her jaw jutted out. Despite her embarrassment, she couldn't let that pass.

"Over my free will? Never!"

Exasperation filled his face.

"Hey, call out the historians. Someone will write a book about you and your courageous principles." His eyes glittered sardonically. "But in the meantime, Emma Valentine, you're coming with me."

SAVE UP TO $30! SIGN UP TODAY!

INSIDE Romance

The complete guide to your favorite
Harlequin®, Silhouette® and Love Inspired® books.

✓ Newsletter ABSOLUTELY FREE! No purchase necessary.

✓ Valuable coupons for future purchases of Harlequin,
  Silhouette and Love Inspired books in every issue!

✓ Special excerpts & previews in each issue. Learn about all
  the hottest titles before they arrive in stores.

✓ No hassle—mailed directly to your door!

✓ Comes complete with a handy shopping checklist
  so you won't miss out on any titles.

- -

SIGN ME UP TO RECEIVE INSIDE ROMANCE
ABSOLUTELY FREE

(Please print clearly)

Name

Address

City/Town   State/Province   Zip/Postal Code

(098 KKM EJL9)

Please mail this form to:
In the U.S.A.: Inside Romance, P.O. Box 9057, Buffalo, NY 14269-9057
In Canada: Inside Romance, P.O. Box 622, Fort Erie, ON L2A 5X3
<u>OR</u> visit http://www.eHarlequin.com/insideromance

IRNBPA06R   ® and ™ are trademarks owned and used by the trademark owner and/or its licensee.

If you enjoyed what you just read,
then we've got an offer you can't resist!

Take 2 bestselling
love stories FREE!
Plus get a FREE surprise gift!

Clip this page and mail it to Harlequin Reader Service®

IN U.S.A.	IN CANADA
3010 Walden Ave.	P.O. Box 609
P.O. Box 1867	Fort Erie, Ontario
Buffalo, N.Y. 14240-1867	L2A 5X3

YES! Please send me 2 free Harlequin® Blaze™ novels and my free surprise gift. After receiving them, if I don't wish to receive anymore, I can return the shipping statement marked cancel. If I don't cancel, I will receive 6 brand-new novels each month, before they're available in stores! In the U.S.A., bill me at the bargain price of $3.99 plus 25¢ shipping and handling per book and applicable sales tax, if any*. In Canada, bill me at the bargain price of $4.47 plus 25¢ shipping and handling per book and applicable taxes**. That's the complete price and a savings of at least 10% off the cover prices—what a great deal! I understand that accepting the 2 free books and gift places me under no obligation ever to buy any books. I can always return a shipment and cancel at any time. Even if I never buy another book from Harlequin, the 2 free books and gift are mine to keep forever.

151 HDN D7ZZ
351 HDN D72D

Name	(PLEASE PRINT)	
Address	Apt.#	
City	State/Prov.	Zip/Postal Code

Not valid to current Harlequin® Blaze™ subscribers.

Want to try two free books from another series?
Call 1-800-873-8635 or visit www.morefreebooks.com.

* Terms and prices subject to change without notice. Sales tax applicable in N.Y.
** Canadian residents will be charged applicable provincial taxes and GST.
   All orders subject to approval. Offer limited to one per household.
® and ™ are registered trademarks owned and used by the trademark owner and/or its licensee.

BLZ05   ©2005 Harlequin Enterprises Limited.

HARLEQUIN®

Blaze™

COMING NEXT MONTH

#273 MY ONLY VICE Elizabeth Bevarly
Rosie Bliss has a little thing for the police chief. Okay, it's more than a *little* thing. But when she propositions the guy, she gets a mixed message. His hands say yes, while his mouth says no. Lucky for her, she's a little hard of hearing….

#274 FEAR OF FALLING Cindi Myers
It Was a Dark And Sexy Night... Bk. 1
As erotic artist John Sartain's business manager, Natalie Brighton has no intention of falling for him…even though something about him fascinates her. But when mysterious things start happening to her, she has to wonder if that fascination is worth her life…

#275 INDULGE Nancy Warren
For a Good Time, Call... Bk. 2
What happens when you eat dessert…before dinner? Mercedes and J. D.'s relationship is only about sex—hot and plenty of it. Suddenly the conservative lawyer wants to change the rules and start over with a *date!* What gives?

#276 JUST TRUST ME... Jacquie D'Alessandro
Adrenaline Rush, Bk. 2
Kayla Watson used to like traveling on business. But that was before her boss insisted she spy on scientist Brett Thorne on his trek into the Andes mountains. Now she's tired, dirty…and seriously in lust with sexy Brett. Lucky for her, he's lusting after her, too. But will it last when he finds out why she's there?

#277 THE SPECIALIST Rhonda Nelson
Men Out of Uniform, Bk. 2
All's fair in love and war. That's Emma Langsford's motto. So when she's given the assignment of recovering a priceless military antique, nothing's going to stop her. And if sexy Brian Payne, aka The Specialist, gets in her way, she has ways of distracting him….

#278 ANYTHING FOR YOU Sarah Mayberry
It's All About Attitude
Delaney Michaels has loved Sam Kirk forever…but the man is too dense to notice! She wants more from life than this, so she's breaking free of Sam to start over. But just as she's making a clean getaway, he counters with a seductive suggestion she can't refuse!

www.eHarlequin.com

HBCNM0806